13 Weird Tales

Sb

bh

A Collection of Original Strange Stories
with Suggestions for Varied Work in English

Paul Groves and Nigel Grimshaw

D1513705

RESOURCE CENTRE
ASHBURTON HIGH SCHOOL
SHIRLEY ROAD
CROYDON, CR9 7AL

Hodder & Stoughton
LONDON SYDNEY AUCKLAND

British Library Cataloguing in Publication Data

Groves, Paul
  13 Weird tales
  1. Readers — 1950 —
 I. Title II. Grimshaw, Nigel
  428'.6   PE1121

  ISBN 0 7131 0174 1

First published 1977
Eleventh impression 1992

© 1977 Paul Groves and Nigel Grimshaw

All rights reserved. No part of this publication may be reproduced or transmitted in any form or by any means, electronic or mechanical, including photocopy, recording, or any information storage and retrieval system, without permission in writing from the publisher or under licence from the Copyright Licensing Agency Limited. Further details of such licences (for reprographic reproduction) may be obtained from the Copyright Licensing Agency Limited, of 90 Tottenham Court Road, London W1P 9HE.

Printed in Great Britain for the educational publishing division of Hodder & Stoughton Ltd, Mill Road, Dunton Green, Sevenoaks, Kent by Athenaeum Press Ltd, Newcastle upon Tyne.

Contents

To the Teacher

The response to *13 Ghosts* has encouraged us to bring out another textbook of similar material about the uncanny, which takes a wider view of the eerie and unnatural. We have included tales of telepathy, premonitions and vampires. There is one ghost here with a peculiarly spectral problem. They have been read and tested in the classroom.

The stories are graded in order of difficulty and the material is slightly harder than that of *13 Ghosts*. To encourage more sustained reading the selection ends with a longer tale. Each story is accompanied by questions which examine first the reader's depth of comprehension and go on to ask about the wider implications of the material and the pupil's experience associated with it. There are questions on language usage and a few exercises on orthography. The final group of questions suggests ideas for various kinds of extended written work, imaginative or more formal. As the questions range from the simple to the more demanding, the book seems suitable for mixed ability classes.

During testing, group prediction was used, in which a section of the story is read and then the group or class is invited to predict the outcome of events from the evidence so far suggested. The stories are, therefore, divided up by + + + + marks suggesting where the teacher might like to pause.

A Dream of Falling

He shouted. Then he was awake. He sat up in bed. Most dreams are hard to remember. This one was not. He could see most of it still and remember most of it.

He had been up in the sky. It was blue and a few clouds moved across it. He rubbed his eyes. Had he seen the sky through a window? Had there been a window in the dream? There had been a strong wind. Had he felt it in his face or had he seen it driving the clouds along? He had been sitting with a friend. That was it. He had been sitting with Bob. Bob had shouted something. He had been laughing. No.

John Elliott got out of bed and switched on the light. He was about sixteen years old. His long hair stood on end and he looked frightened. He sat in a chair and smoothed back his hair. Then he put his face in his hands and stared at nothing.

Bob had been laughing and talking. But that was at the start of the dream. They had been strapped in their seats. If he put his hands over his eyes, he could see Bob in the dream again. He saw his grin. He could see something smooth, painted white with blue marks on it. Would that have been the wing of an aeroplane? Yes, that was it. In the dream he had been flying somewhere with Bob.

They were travelling at speed. He could feel the speed pulling at them as they turned in the air. Then they were diving.

+ + + +

John Elliott opened his eyes wide with fear and swallowed. That was what had wakened him. A dream of falling. They had dived. Then everything had started to shake and jerk. He had been thrown from his seat and Bob with him. They were falling through the air. Falling.

In most dreams of falling you wake before you hit the bottom. In this one, he had not wakened up. He had hit. Very hard. There had been a bright light, a sharp pain and then blackness.

But it was not the pain that had made him wake up and shout. It was the nothingness after the blackness came in the dream. That nothingness had gone on for a long time. A very long time. It had gone on so long that he could not stand it. Then he had wakened up and shouted.

+ + + +

After a while he went back to bed and read a book. But his mind kept wandering. He turned out the light and tried to sleep. But he heard the hours strike all through the rest of the night.

'You look a bit pale, John,' his mother said at breakfast. 'Don't you feel well?'

'I didn't sleep,' he said. 'I had a dream of falling.'

'You'll have to watch your step today, then.' His father grinned at him.

'Not that kind of falling,' he said. 'I was in a plane, I think. There was a crash.'

'Well, you're not likely to be in a real plane,' his father said. 'I only wish we could afford it.'

'Don't worry about it,' his mother told him. 'Dreams don't come true.'

'I hope not,' John said.

+ + + +

But he could not stop thinking about it. Maybe it meant something. Did dreams foretell the future? The thought made him ask Bob at break, 'Where are you going for your holidays this year?'

'Down to Cornwall. Dad's got a caravan hired on a site.'

'You're not having a package holiday as well? You're not

flying anywhere?'

'Some hopes. Wish we were. Why?'

'I had a dream about flying. You were with me and there was an accident.'

'A dream? So what?' Bob laughed. 'Dreams don't mean anything.'

'I feel that this one did mean something.'

'Daft,' Bob said.

+ + + +

So he could not talk to Bob about it. After school he hung about outside the travel agency. At last he got the courage and went in. There were two girls behind the counter.

'Can I help you?' one of them said.

'Do any airlines have colours on their planes in white and blue?' he asked.

'I think so.' She stared at him. 'Jill? Some airlines do, don't they?'

'I'm not quite sure,' said the other girl, Jill. 'I have an idea that Air France do. I think TWA are white and blue. Why?'

'No reason.' He felt himself go red. 'I just wanted to know.'

+ + + +

Outside he remembered their faces and felt silly. The whole thing was silly. If the dream did mean something, he would never know. It would do him no good to know. He could not write to Air France or TWA and say that a blue and white plane was going to crash. They would ask him which one. How did he know? If he told them he had had a dream, they would think he was crazy. Anyway, he would not be going anywhere on a plane.

So he put it out of his mind. It lingered a bit in odd moments until the week-end but then he forgot it altogether. He packed in the football the following week. That gave him something to think about. He had quite a quarrel with the lads about it. But he had started to go out

3

with Maureen Palmer. Bob had picked up first with her friend Lesley Hill. At first John went with them to make up the four. But he quite liked Maureen. The four of them went out together a lot in the next two weeks. They had a lot of fun.

+ + + +

They had been looking forward to the October fair. On the Saturday night they went down together. It was a blaze of lights and a blare of music. They all went on the Dodgems, ate hot dogs and rolled a few pennies. It was Bob who suggested the Gliderama.

'It's twenty-five pence each tonight,' John said. He looked at the excited faces circling round. It was not the money. He had an uncomfortable feeling about it.

'You're scared,' Bob told him.

'Don't talk wet,' John told him. 'Come on, Maureen.'

But, for some reason the girls wanted to sit together and he and Bob shared a machine.

+ + + +

It was only on the third trip round that John knew where the feeling had come from. As they went round faster and faster, the thing they sat in was flung further and further out, tilting. The whole roundabout tilted to give the feeling of flying. What they sat in was a cylinder with a small tail and short, stubby wings. It was painted blue and white.

The memory of the dream was freezingly clear in his mind.

'We've got to get out!' He grabbed Bob's arm.

'We can't. Going too fast. Scared?' Bob grinned at him.

'There's going to be an accident. I had a dream.'

'A dream? And you're scared of that? Wait till I tell the girls after.' And Bob laughed.

That was almost the last thing John heard. As the tiny plane was right at the top of its swing, the bolts that held it parted. There was hardly time for anyone to scream. It fell with a crash on the concrete parking space beyond the stalls.

The screams came a moment later. A crowd with shocked, white faces gathered. A doctor came. Bob lived for an hour in hospital. John had been killed almost instantly as his neck was broken.

That was his mother's only comfort. At least the police said so. A policewoman was sent to tell her.

'It was very sudden,' she said. 'He wouldn't have known anything. It would have been too quick. Things like that happen without any warning at all.'

Think It Over

Where is John Elliott when the story starts?
What has he been dreaming about? Who is with him in the dream?
Did he find it easy to sleep afterwards? Why?
How do you know that the dream was still affecting him the following day?
What kind of reaction did he get from his parents when he told them about the dream?
Who else did he tell?
What did he do about the dream after that?
For how long afterwards did he go on thinking about the dream?
At what season of the year was the fair held?
When did he first realise that his dream was connected with the fair? Give some evidence for what you say.
What was the cause of the accident?

Do You Know?

Give another title for the story.
Have you ever had nightmares? In your opinion what causes them?
What are clouds made of? Why do they move?
When human beings are frightened, does their hair stand on

end? Have you ever seen it? You can tell how animals feel by the way their fur lies. Can you give some instances?

Have you ever had a dream that you were falling? Can you give the medical explanation for this?

What do you do when you cannot sleep? Some people count sheep. This is rather old-fashioned. Suggest a more modern method.

Do dreams have a meaning? If you think they do, give some examples from your own experience.

Do you always go to the same place for your holidays? Where have you been during the past five years? How many in your class spend holidays at home? At some place in Great Britain? Abroad?

October fair ... January sales. Can you think of any other events connected with months?

Have you ever been up in a plane? What is usually the most frightening time in an air trip?

What colours does British Airways use? Lufthansa? Air France?

Do you have a local fair? List the machines that you can ride on. Which gives the most enjoyable ride? Which is the most scaring?

What do you feel is the worst thing a policeman or woman has to do?

What do you think of the policewoman's remark to John's mother? Do you think people get a warning about what is to happen? Have you any experience of such things?

Would anyone be to blame for the accident? Why?

Name one thing in John's dream which was quite unlike the reality of the accident.

Using Words

'Can I help you?' What other ways are there of greeting someone who enters a shop?

'You look a bit pale' What other terms are used to tell a person he looks ill?

'Watch your step'. How many ways can you think of saying 'Take care'?

Nothingness . . . blackness. Write down ten words ending in -ness.

' . . . he was crazy' Give some other ways of saying this.

Punctuate the speech in the following. Then, check your version with the story.

> you look a bit pale john his mother said at breakfast don't you feel well i didn't sleep he said i had a dream of falling you'll have to watch your step today then his father grinned at him

How many question marks are there in the story?

'If the dream did mean something, he would never know.' Complete the following:

> If you drive too fast on icy roads, . . .
> If the boy had got up earlier, . . .
> If England had a warmer climate, . . .
> If you do not speak clearly, . . .

The fair is described as 'a blaze of lights and a blare of music'. In a few sentences, describe a disco or a wood in summer.

A feeling that something is about to happen is a premon . . .

Make a list of all the words you can think of in which 'al' is joined to another word. Make sure you spell them correctly.

Write Now

Write a story about a real plane crash.

A prisoner waiting to be shot hears all the hours of the night strike. What goes through his mind? You have to see the headmaster on the following day for something you have done and you cannot sleep at night. What goes through your mind? Write one of these stories.

Make a list of all the airlines you know.

Write a poem called 'Falling' or 'Fairground'.

You go on a ghost train at a fair and find yourself in another world. Write the story.

Imagine that you are either an air hostess or an airline pilot. Write a diary of a day at work.

In play-form write down what the girls in the travel agency say when John has gone out.

Oboe to Control

On the way down in the car, Alison had felt happy and excited. As soon as they reached the holiday site, she felt dreadful. It grew worse when they drove up to the caravan and worse still when they were inside.

'What's up, Alison?' her father asked. 'You don't look too good.'

'I can smell burning,' she said. Her mother sniffed the air.

'Nonsense,' she said cheerfully. 'All you can smell is newness. This place is brand new. Look at it. It's better than I'd hoped. Look at all these cupboards. Get the stuff out of the car and I'll make us all a cup of tea. You'd like a cup, Jack, wouldn't you?'

'Not half,' he said. 'It was boiling in that car coming down.'

It was more a mobile home than a caravan. Bright paint shone everywhere. Sunlight gleamed on shining metal. They were obviously the first people to use the place. And yet, Alison had this feeling.

+ + + +

She had had these feelings before; once in a room in an old house. Twice, in two old churches. There had been other times. But they had not been quite like this. Other people never had such feelings. At first she had talked about them. But she had been laughed at and she had learned better.

This time it was different. She was not only afraid; she was waiting for something to happen. She had to wait. She knew that.

Her mother made a cup of tea. They sat around and chatted about what they were going to do and Alison tried to join in. Later they had something to eat. Everyone was glad to be away on holiday. Then her Dad and her brother, Steve, went out to play with a ball while Alison washed up with her mother. And Alison did not speak of what she felt. What use would it have been? It would only have spoiled things for the others. And all the time she had this sense of something frightening and sad, smouldering away, ready to happen.

Darkness fell. She went to bed. She heard a faint buzz of talk from her parents at the other end of the caravan. Then they went to bed. She listened to Steve's quiet, relaxed breathing from the other bunk. He murmured in his sleep. Time passed. The place was very quiet. She heard a night bird and a faint breeze breathed on the window. But she could not sleep.

+ + + +

She was waiting for something and it came at last. At first it was a faint crackling which she thought was the noise of a fire. When she heard the voice, she realised it was radio static. The pilot of a plane was talking to the ground.

'Oboe to Control,' it said. 'Oboe to Control. Control. Oh, God. Control!' The man sounded very tired and very scared. She could almost see the hopelessness in his eyes. There was more crackling. Then another voice, a firmer one, said, 'Control to Oboe. Receiving you, strength five. Come in, Oboe.'

'We're on fire. Badly shot up. I can't get the undercart down. Prepare for crash landing.'

She heard rapid muttering in the background and the firmer voice spoke again. 'We're ready for you, Oboe. You're cleared to land. Over.'

'I can see the field. We're coming in.'

'How many hurt?'

'Two dead. Jones bought it over the target. I'm a bit shot

up. An engine's gone.'

It was not a dream. Alison could see the pale squares of the windows. Outside them the cloudless sky held nothing but stars. She could hear someone murmur again in their sleep. The sheet was smooth against her chin. And the dreadful voices spoke to no one but themselves and her.

'Oboe to Control!'

'Control.'

'I'm not going to make it on this run in. She's hard to handle.' There was a gasp. 'Christ! She's not answering the stick now. God help us. We've had it. Oh, God! God! God!'

+ + + +

The last word became a scream. Then there was a terrifying, tearing, crunching sound that seemed to fill the whole world. Before it ended, there was the boom of an explosion and an intense and savage crackle of fiercely burning flames.

She could not even cry out. And then, when it had all ended, she fell into a sleep as deep and as black as the silence that came.

The following morning, they told her that she looked pale. But she did not tell them why. What would have been the point? Besides, the voices meant that she had to do something. No one could help her with that. She would have to find out for herself what she was meant to do. The burning pilot in the plane had been crying out to her.

+ + + +

Without saying where she was going, she went off quietly by herself, after breakfast. She walked inland and soon came to a village. It dozed quietly in the sun. The red tiles of its roofs glowed in the morning light and two pigeons perched on an ivy-covered wall. The world was full of easiness and warmth. It only made what she had heard at night more real and more dreadful.

At the end of the street, she could see the church spire. She walked towards it. She said, 'Good morning' to two old men who greeted her. She came to the churchyard.

The walls of the church were knobbly with flints and over the wall she could see several small white gravestones. Some had names that looked Polish. Most of them, though, were English. The dates were 1943 and 1944. She opened the lych gate and went up the path.

+ + + +

After the brightness outside, it was cool and dim in the church but she hardly noticed the change. She felt like a sleepwalker; it was as if something had taken over her mind and was guiding her. With a quick glance round to see that she was alone, she went directly to a table. Red-backed books lay on it. In a smooth movement, she picked one up, hid it under her pullover and walked out of the church.

That night, lying in bed in the darkness, she felt how strange it had been. She had gone straight back to the caravan. She had hardly looked at the notice on the door—'Alison: we've gone to the beach. Follow us down.' In a dazed way, she had gone into the van, pushed the prayer book out of sight under her pillow and gone straight out again. During the day, she had almost forgotten the book and even the happenings of the night had not been so sharp in her mind.

Now, everyone around her was fast asleep. The hours had gone by and the voices were coming back. She had brought the torch from the car. She switched it on now under the bedclothes and opened the book. She did not know what she was looking for.

+ + + +

The radio static was in her ears once more. Then the voice. 'Oboe to Control. Oboe to Control. Control!'

The tears were running down her cheeks. She could hardly see the words on the page. Only the bold capitals at the top stood out. AT THE BURIAL OF THE DEAD. She sniffed, wiped her eyes and began to read half way down the page. There was a lot to read.

She read it to the end even though this night was different from the last. The voices repeated what they had said until the pilot in the burning plane said, 'I can see the field. We're coming in.' Then he stopped. She heard him draw a long struggling breath. 'Ah!' he whispered. His voice was full of relief. 'At last.' It was calmer, almost peaceful and somehow grateful. 'Safe, now,' he whispered. 'Free, thank God. We're home.'

There were no more voices. She read on and her tears dried. She knew now that she had done the one thing that was right. The only sound to break the silence was the murmur of her own voice under the covers. She felt flooded with peace. When the service was ended, she crept out of the van and stood on the moist, cool grass.

The sky was cloudless, a maze of stars. A gentle breeze lifted her hair. The pain and the heaviness and terror had left her. Her sleep, when she stumbled back to bed, was like a blessing.

The next morning she woke late, but she was still filled with that quiet happiness. She heard voices and looked out of the door of the van. There was a man with her father.

'My daughter, Alison,' he said. 'This is Mr Langton.'

'How do you do?' Mr Langton nodded. 'I'm the site manager.' He turned back to his talk with her father. 'Yes. During the war this was a bomber field. Must have been some tense moments here at times. As I hear tell, where your caravan is now is where the radio—er—the tower—er'

'The Control Tower,' Alison suddenly realised.

'That's right.' He stared at her slightly surprised. Then he made as if to move on. 'Still,' he said, 'that's all over now. It's peaceful enough now, this morning, isn't it?' He looked up at the shining blue. Skylarks were going up, singing.

'Yes,' she said. 'It's all at peace now.' She was sure of it.

Think It Over

When did Alison start to feel unhappy?
What did she find odd about the caravan?
Where before had she had strange feelings about places she
   had visited?
Why could she not sleep?
What did she think the strange noise was at first? Then what
   did she realise?
How do you know from almost the first words he says that
   the pilot is frightened?
How did Alison know that she was not dreaming?
Why did she go to the church?
Where did she put the prayer book when she got back to the
   caravan?
How did she feel when she heard the ghostly pilot again?
   How do you know?
What told her that she had done the right thing?
How did she feel when she woke up on the following
   morning?
Whom did she meet?
Why did Alison hear voices in that particular spot?

Do You Know?

Why was it that none of the others in the caravan could
   smell burning?
What is the difference between a caravan and a mobile
   home?
'All you can smell is newness.' How does 'newness' smell?
   What kinds of smells do you think are pleasant? How can
   you describe them? What is your favourite smell?
Have you ever been in a place about which you had strange
   feelings? Describe your experience.
Name two night birds.

Alison does not mention how she feels. Should you always say what you feel? Are there times when it is better to keep quiet? What is your experience?

What is the 'undercart' on a plane? What is 'static' on a radio? What causes it? Can you find out?

Why is it necessary to have an air traffic control tower at an airport? What kind of work does an air traffic control officer do?

The ghost plane was on a bombing raid during the last war. Can you name some of the bombers that were used then? What are the names of some bombing planes of today?

How badly injured do you think the pilot is?

Why do you think Alison slept after her experience?

Do you think that ghosts are trying to contact people to tell them things? Or is it all imagination?

Was Alison stealing the prayer book? Why?

In many areas houses are built of local stone. What is the local stone in your area? Or are the houses built of brick? If so, what does this tell you about your local stone as a building material? Can you tell from the way the church is built what part of this country Alison is in?

'We're home.' Why do you think the ghost pilot says this? What does he mean?

Are there any wartime airfields near you? What are they now used for?

Why might some of the gravestones in the churchyard have had Polish names on them?

Do you think Alison enjoyed the rest of her holiday? Why?

Using Words

'You don't look too good.' What other ways are there of saying this?

'Not half.' What does this mean? Do you say it? Or is it only older people who use it?

'Over', 'Over and out.' Who uses phrases like this? What do they mean? What does 'Strength five' mean? If you do not know, can you guess?

'Jones bought it.' This is a less straightforward way of saying, 'Jones is dead.' Can you give some other phrases which mean the same thing?

'She's not answering the stick.' What is the 'stick'? How many other special words or phrases can you think of connected with flying?

Copy out two violent sentences from the story and two peaceful ones.

Describe grass with dew on it in a sentence which shows exactly how the dew looked.

'He drew a long struggling breath.' What other word can you suggest besides 'struggling' to show the way he was breathing?

'Spoil' How many words can you think of with 'oi' in them?

Write Now

Write an account of what happened on the bombing raid.

You are a passenger on an airplane and something goes wrong. Write a description of what happens. *OR* Write a story called 'The Holiday that Went Wrong'.

In a few sentences describe a big explosion of any kind.

Write a poem called 'Flames in the Night' or 'The Old Church'.

Design a lay-out for the interior of your ideal caravan.

The Hitch Hiker

James Stephens had been driving for three hours. The rain which had started as he left home had poured down all that time. Normally he liked driving in the dark. But he did not like it in rain; and it was heavy rain at that.

The windscreen wipers had kept up their hypnotic 'swish-swish' making a tune in his brain. His fear was that they would send him to sleep. Every now and then he had felt his head drop forward and he had to keep pulling it up to look at the road.

What he needed was a cup of coffee. But he knew that on this route nowhere was open at this time of night. He was glad, therefore, when he saw the hitch-hiker.

A white arm had thumbed him out of the darkness. He did not normally pick up hitch-hikers even in the daytime, let alone at night. But he felt the risk was worth taking. It would be somebody to talk to; somebody who could keep him awake.

+ + + +

He braked fairly quickly. Even so he must have come to a stop about a hundred metres past the hitch-hiker. It would take him a few seconds to run up; more if he had a heavy pack.

He opened the nearside door for him and lit a cigarette. He assumed it was a him. It could be a her, of course.

He waited. Some rain drifted in. To his surprise he saw no one. Yet he could have sworn he heard running feet. It must have been rain beating on the car.

Had he really seen a hitch-hiker? Perhaps it was just a trick played by his lights. They could do that sometimes.

Make you see things that weren't there. Still no one came. He shut the door and drove on. The air from the open door had wakened him. He drove hard.

+ + + +

He had gone three or four miles through very lonely country. No other traffic was on the road. Then he got this feeling that he was not alone in the car. It was silly really but he got the feeling of a presence other than himself. There was no shape or sound but he got this feeling. He kept looking at the passenger seat. Nothing was there. He felt silly for looking but he had to keep looking because the feeling was so strong.

His heart was beating faster. This was a very lonely stretch of road. Because of this he did not want to stop. Besides, what could he find if he did stop? His brain must be over-tired. He must put his foot down and get to the next town and get a cup of coffee.

It was then that he sensed something else besides his own hands gripping the wheel. As well as his own now tightly-gripped hands, something else was there. And it was pulling him to the left. He was going to crash! He was going to crash, if he did not control this thing pulling him off the road.

He fought to control the wheel in a cold sweat. But the thing was stronger. He must crash!

+ + + +

Just as he thought his end had come, a side road appeared and they were suddenly off the main road and going down this minor road.

The thing had now relaxed its grip of the wheel and he was in control again. At all costs he must get back on the main road and into the nearest town. He would turn right at the next turn.

His lights caught a signpost pointing right. He slowed but once more the thing gripped the wheel and guided him straight on. Yes, that was it. He was being guided somewhere. But where?

What thing would get in his car and guide him somewhere? What was the purpose? It could not be for his good. Something evil was going to happen to him. At all costs he must stop the car as soon as he saw some house. At least this thing could not control the pedals. Or could it?

The road was twisty but the thing gripping the wheel seemed to know every bend. If he had dared, he could have taken his hands off the wheel. There must be a house or a cottage soon—some light. But no, the narrow road went on and on.

+ + + +

Then he did see a light in the distance. Would the road go by it? Was it a cottage or better still a pub? The headlights suddenly shone on the wall of the building. He jammed his foot on the brake and skidded to a halt.

He leapt out of the car and ran towards the light. He was expecting to hear footsteps following him but his breathing was heavy. He hammered on a door. He stood hanging on to the knocker and listening to his breathing. Would someone come?

To his relief he heard bolts being shot back and the door opened. An old woman stood there. 'Let me in for God's sake!' he yelled. 'And shut the door quickly!'

The old woman smiled. 'How nice to see you, son,' she said. 'Come in out of the wet.'

He rushed past her into a room full of old furniture. It was like rushing into another age.

'Wipe your feet, son,' he heard from the hall. But he was too frightened to go back. He fell into a chair and was relieved to hear the door being shut and bolted.

+ + + +

The old woman came in to him. She was wrinkled and white-haired. She looked quite calm. She had not caught his fear as most women would have. 'Best shut out the night,' she said. 'Would you like a cup of tea?'

He worried what she was thinking of him. Did she think of him as some madman who had burst in on her out of the night? Did she think he needed calming down? 'Yes, please,' he said. 'I've had a shock.'

'I'll put the kettle on. Won't be a jiffy.' She went into what he took to be the kitchen. He felt now able to look round the room, though he was listening all the time for the door.

+ + + +

As he had first noticed the room looked odd. The radio was old. A newspaper by it was twenty years out of date, yet it still looked crisp and new. That was it. Although the room was out-of-date, many of the things in it looked newish.

She came back in to him. 'He'll be down in a minute,' she said.

'Who?' he asked.

She smiled at him and poured out the tea.

He looked at her. What he had taken for calmness was a far-away look in her eyes. Her body was with him in the room but her eyes were not.

'He likes the driver to have a cup of tea,' she said. 'On a wet night like this it's bad for hitch-hiking. It was good of you to pick him up.'

For a moment he did not take in what she had said. 'I didn't pick anyone up. I stopped but there was no one there. I came here because I had a frightening experience.'

The old woman smiled. 'I tell him to go by the train but he will hitch-hike. Luckily, good souls like yourself pick him up. I was worried till I saw you both at the door.'

+ + + +

He dropped the cup he had just picked up.

'Hark, he's coming down now.'

He could hear footsteps on the stairs. He ran for the door. As he bent to undo the bolts he felt a hand on his shoulder. He swung round to aim a blow but then the bolts gave to his other hand and he was out into the night.

He tumbled into his car and turned the key. The engine

choked but would not start. He turned the key repeatedly but there was only the whirring of the starter motor. He saw a white arm coming down the path from the cottage. It came closer till it pressed against the side window. The old woman was with it. 'Can we help?' she said. He leapt from the car and ran.

+ + + +

After a week the police connected the man in the hospital with the car they had found left in a country lane. The doctors told the man he was James Stephens in an attempt to get his memory working again. The police had found him five miles from his car. He was muddy, soaked through, and unable to speak.

'Funny his car was found there,' said the sergeant at the police station. 'Do you remember that old woman who committed suicide at that cottage the night her son was killed hitch-hiking? Just back on the main road he was knocked down.'

'No,' said the constable, 'must have been before my time.'

'Yes, I suppose it was,' said the sergeant. 'Must go back at least twenty years. No one's lived there since. Now what would cause a man to leave his car there and lose his memory?'

'They say you can lose your memory, if you don't want to remember something,' said the younger man.

'You read too many books,' said the sergeant.

Think It Over

Why might James Stephens not have liked driving in the rain?

What were his reasons for wanting to pick up the hitch-hiker?

Why was he more awake when he drove on?

When did he first really know that he was not alone in the car?

How did he realise that the thing in the car was taking him
somewhere?

Why might turning right get him back on the main road?

Why would a pub have been a better place to reach than a
cottage?

At first, whom do you think the old woman is speaking to
when she says, 'son'?

What made him feel safe, when he first came into the
cottage?

How did the old woman react to his rushing into the house?
What does this tell you?

'He'll be down in a minute.' Who is the 'he'?

What might have prevented the car from starting?

Why, do you think, he had been taken to the cottage?

Do You Know?

How many inches of rain fall, on average, in your area in a
year?

How do you know when you are tired? Does travelling on a
bus, in a train, or in a car send some people to sleep?
Do any of these send you to sleep? What causes the
sleep in such cases? What sort of regular sounds cause
sleep?

Does coffee help to keep a person awake? Is there a scientific
cause for it or not? Do you know?

Would you pick up a hitch-hiker, if you drove a car? Are
there any reasons against it? Why should girls be wary of
it?

From where you are sitting, name something one hundred
metres away.

What is meant by a sixth sense? Can you give an instance
from your own experience?

Skidding. Why do cars skid? Why did this car skid to a halt?
What is the way to correct a skid in a moving car? Have
you ever been in a bad skid?

Have you ever felt you were not alone? If so what
   happened?
What is the loneliest place you have been to?
Which pedal in a car with hand gears is the brake?
Why does the old woman not really see James Stephens?
   What time is it in the room? What year?
Why should the ghostly presence only be an arm? Has this
   something to do with the crash the woman's son was in?
Do people forget things they don't want to remember?
   What is your experience?

Using Words

A repeated sound that sends you to sleep can be called
   hypn. . . .
'A white arm thumbed him.' How many short sentences can
   you think up using words from the hands or feet as verbs?
   Can you use: palmed, fingered, toed, knuckled?
'Some rain drifted in.' Was it a windy night or not?
Describe in a few sentences how the rain would have come
   in on a night of high wind.
'It was silly really.' What other ways could you say this?
'Put his foot down.' Here it means to accelerate or go faster.
   What else would 'I must put my foot down about this,'
   mean?
'He must crash!' Why is the exclamation mark used there?
What is the full name for: a pub, a plane and a bike?
On a door you can have a lock, a bolt or a handle. What do
   you have on a gate?
'I won't be a jiffy.' How many other ways can you think of
   saying this?
'He did not take in what she had said.' Explain the
   differences between these by using them in a sentence:
   take in and intake; take over and overtake; take up and
   uptake.

'Somebody' Make a list of 'some' words. Make sure you put in the 'e'.

To suffer from loss of memory is called amn. . . .

Write Now

Is a ghost necessarily evil? Can you have good ghosts? Write about a friendly one who helps someone.

In a few sentences describe something odd you see as a passenger in the headlights of a car.

Have you ever tried hitch-hiking? Give an account of any experience if you have.

If you went back twenty years in time what sort of changes would you notice in clothes or anything else?

Have you ever been out walking or camping at night? What sort of things did you find frightening?

Is there an old house or ruined building near you? If so, write a story about it.

From the few clues given describe the police sergeant.

In play-form write about two nurses talking about the case of James Stephens with the young policeman.

A Ghostly Problem

The Brant Manor ghosts had a problem. For years Mr Spook had haunted the Manor. He was a hard-working ghost who always kept to his proper hours: twelve till two in the morning. He was not like some young ghosts who turn up after midnight, or go on strike because it is too hot, or knock off for five minutes for a quick smoke.

He was also very good at his trade; he knew how to scare people. He had studied this art from his father, now retired. His ghostly moan was very good: long, low and chilling to humans. One American tourist had rushed home by the next plane after hearing it.

He could drag his left foot too and make a bumping sound. On special days, around Christmas time, he was an expert at chain dragging. This feature of his art was in all the books about the Manor; it attracted ghost hunters from all over the world.

Walking through walls was no trouble to him. His favourite trick was to appear through the panelled wall of the old Duke's bedroom, walk along the corridor, bump down the stairs, and disappear through the bookshelves of the library.

But perhaps his speciality was the head-under-the-arm business. He was well known and respected by his fellow ghosts because not only could he carry his head under his arm, but he could make it grin too. This had taken years of practice which no modern ghost would do. The hard bit was to get the lips to turn up at the corners because a ghost's lips naturally turn down.

+ + + +

As haunting takes place late at night, a ghost can get very tired. But so that the tradition could be kept up, when Mr Spook was too tired Mrs Spook took his place. She was not as good as he was, because she was part-time, as it were. She could certainly not manage the head-under-the-arm business, but she did have a speciality, which was a quick glide down the long corridor without her feet touching the floor. This caused people's hair to stand on end. And when she passed right through them they usually fainted. So she too had a reputation.

+ + + +

To these two honest, hard-working, professional ghosts came a happy event: a baby ghost was born. It was late in death too, some three hundred years after they had died. Never had a baby such loving care and, as soon as he could toddle, Dad Spook started to teach him the business. First the low chilling moan and then how to pass through walls. The young ghost picked it up splendidly and Mr and Mrs Spook were very proud of him.

+ + + +

When he was seven years old his great night dusked. He was to go on his first haunting. He was to be allowed to appear through the old Duke's bedroom and give his low, chilling moan. A party of American tourists was expected. This could give them a real thrill: a new ghost at the Manor.

Dad and Mum Spook proudly watched him set off and waited to hear the screams of the Americans. They heard screams all right, great sobbing screams coming from their beloved son as he rushed back through the wall. 'What is the matter, son?' asked Dad, picking him up. The matter was that son did not like the dark.

+ + + +

Thus the Brant Manor ghosts had a problem. Son was all right in the dark with his parents because of the ghostly glow from their bodies. But on his own, no!

The doctor was called. A rare case he declared. He could

deal with sore throats and heats but not this sort of thing. The boy might grow out of it in a hundred years or so.

Mr and Mrs Spook became more and more sorrowful as the years went by and their son did not improve. Who would take over when Dad retired? Brant Manor had never been without a ghost. Then one day Mum thought of Uncle Ebenezer who haunted a castle in Scotland. He had often expressed a wish to see the boy.

The family borrowed a phantom stage coach from a local inn and set off, Son clinging to his mother because he had never left the Manor before.

Uncle Ebenezer met them on the long staircase and greeted them all as coldly as he could. He had a special chilling hug and kiss for Son.

In the Green Study Uncle Ebenezer was obviously deeply moved by the problem; he took off his head to think about it. Then he ruffled his hair with his long bony fingers. 'I have it,' he said, his sockets lighting up, 'the boy must have a light!'

'A light?' exclaimed Dad. 'No self-respecting ghost has a light.'

'There is a precedent for it, I assure you,' said Uncle Ebenezer. 'We have a Lady Macbeth up here who haunts a castle with a candle. It is all perfectly respectable. I think I have the very thing.' From an old oak trunk he produced a two-foot-long candle. 'Try this,' he said.

+ + + +

Back at the Manor Mum and Dad Spook waited tensely as Son went through the bedroom wall with his candle. Soon there were screams. Not ghostly screams but human screams from the occupant of the bed. Son came back looking green with delight. 'Can I do it again?' he asked. Mum and Dad looked at each other proudly.

Now the books on Brant Manor record a third ghost. It appears earlier than the other two (young ghosts must not lose too much sleep) and haunts the bedroom with a mysterious light. None of the experts can understand why.

Think It Over

What were Mr Spook's working hours?

Who had taught him how to haunt?

Whom had his moaning scared particularly? How can you tell?

What was his particular trick at Christmas time?

What was his speciality?

What was Mrs Spook's speciality?

What did she do to make people faint?

How long had the ghosts been haunting before the young ghost was born?

What was the young ghost first taught?

Who did all the screaming on the young ghost's first night and why?

What was the ghostly problem?

What reassurance did the doctor offer?

What worried them most about the problem?

How did they travel to Scotland?

What was ghostly about Uncle Ebenezer's hug?

What remedy did Uncle Ebenezer offer?

How did he deal with the Spooks' objections?

How did his parents know that the young Spook was delighted with his success?

What can the experts not understand about the third ghost at Brant Manor?

Do You Know?

What is being poked fun at in the first paragraph?

What do you think about comic ghost stories? Does comedy spoil a ghost story?

Do you have any favourite programmes or cartoons about ghosts on TV?

What is the traditional time for ghosts to disappear? (Mr

Spook worked shorter hours than most.)

What is the name of the society that investigates ghostly happenings?

Do you know any stories in which a ghost appears through a wall? Why might it do this?

Where do ghosts go in the day time? Do ghosts only appear at night?

Why might a ghost's lips naturally turn down?

Is there any reason why the young ghost started at seven years old?

Do you know any superstitions connected with numbers?

How do you know Uncle Ebenezer is a skeleton?

Who was Lady Macbeth? Who wrote a play about her?

Borley Rectory, a real place, was famous because it was haunted. Can you name any other places that are famous for their ghosts?

Who is the famous female ghost that walks in the Tower of London with her head tucked underneath her arm?

Using Words

'Turn up' in this story means 'to appear'. Put it in a sentence.

Can you also put these in sentences: turn out, turn in, turn over?

'Walking through walls was no trouble to him.' Complete these sentences:

 Driving in snow is . . .

 Helping in the garden can be . . .

 Walking in the country in summer is . . .

'Late in death'; 'the great night dusked'. What are the normal phrases used?

'Toddle' describes how a baby walks. How many other words can you think of that describe the way a person walks? Make a list.

'What's the matter?' How many ways can you think of saying this?

'He could deal with sore throats and heats.' What would a human being have instead of a 'heat'?

'There is a precedent for it, I assure you.' How would you say the same thing, if you were talking to a friend of yours?

'Speciality' How many words can you think of ending in 'ity'? Can you get six?

Make a list of words that rhyme with 'scare'. Put them under these headings: 'are' words; 'air' words; and 'ear' words.

Think up a good name for two ghosts: Mr . . . and Mrs . . .

Make up a name for the young ghost in this story.

Copy out the words using a hyphen in this story. Can you explain why any of them have it?

Write Now

Write a poem called 'The Phantom Stage Coach'.

In play-form. The occupant of the bed describes his experience when he gets back to America.

Write a section for a guide book about the ghosts of Brant Manor. Seriously.

Write part of a script for your favourite TV ghost cartoon. Make it funny.

What do they call a ghost that haunts pubs? An Inn Spectre. Write down any joke you know about a ghost.

Describe in a few sentences how Uncle Ebenezer haunts his Scottish castle.

The Wild Children

The dark forest surrounded the little village. It stretched away for miles. That day all the villagers were in the village square. No one had ever seen anything like the wood children. Max, the forester, had caught them.

The two children spoke no human language. They were very brown, dirty and wore rags. Max had tied their hands together and tied them by another rope round their necks to a post. A cloth was wrapped round his hand where one of them had bitten him. The children chattered like monkeys, showing their sharp, white teeth. If anyone went too near them they would snap and spit at him. Their eyes were not human, either. They blazed like the eyes of wild animals.

+ + + +

'What are you going to do with them, Max?' a villager asked.

'I don't know.' He shook his head.

'I'll take them.'

The villagers turned round. A cart had drawn up. Jorg, the travelling showman, was driving it. He was a big man, with a thick red neck and small eyes above a cruel mouth.

'You?' Max looked at him.

'Me,' snapped Jorg. 'I'll take 'em.'

Max looked at the white horse, whose bones stuck through its skin. In the back of the cart was a cringing dog. It looked more starved than the horse.

'No. Don't let him have them!' It was the village priest who had spoken and Jorg glared at him with a snarl.

'You shut your mouth,' Jorg growled.

'I've heard of you,' the priest accused him. 'You and your

trained animals. They don't last long when you have them.'

'Mind your own business,' Jorg snarled.

'That little hunchback you had who used to dance so that you could collect money. What happened to her?' the priest went on.

'That sickly thing. She died.' Jorg laughed shortly.

'You can't let him have them.' The priest appealed to Max.

'Look at 'em,' Max said. 'They're like animals. Who else would have them? Would you?'

Sadly, the priest shook his head.

'Come on, then,' Jorg cried. 'I haven't got all day.' He took out a bag of coins and shook it. 'How much for 'em?'

'Let them go,' the priest pleaded. Max looked at him doubtfully.

'Let them go?' Jorg shouted. 'Who knows what evil they'll get up to back in those forests? Don't talk stupid. I'll keep 'em safe. I can make good use of them when I've got them caged up. How much?'

Max named a price. He and Jorg argued about it. Then the boys were sold. The priest said no more.

+ + + +

Jorg hauled the two wild children into the cart and bound them tight by their necks. Then he drove off, their two heads bobbing painfully against the back rail of the cart.

His cottage was two miles away on the fringe of the forest. Outside it stood a gaily painted wagon. On it a sign said 'Jorg Wolfar: Come and See the Trained Animals and Wonders in the Side Shows.' There were cages outside the cottage. In one a small brown bear whimpered and made itself small as Jorg went by. In another a large cat flattened itself on the ground as he passed.

His sister, Gisel, was inside the cottage. She was making a young dog do tricks. It did not please her. She grabbed its leg and threw it across the room. It yelped and licked itself, its thin sides trembling.

'Come and see what I've got,' Jorg told her. Gisel was older than her brother and even uglier. But her face lit up and her broken teeth showed in a smile when she saw the two small boys.

'They'll make us a bit of money, those will,' she hissed.

'They'll need taming, first,' Jorg grunted. He dragged them to a cage and threw them in.

'Never fear,' she told him. 'We'll tame 'em, won't we? Like before. You beat 'em and I'll starve 'em.'

When, after he had eaten, he took his whip and went out, she sniggered. Hearing it crack and the squeals of the wild children, she cackled with joy and clapped her podgy hands together.

+ + + +

Three days later, the wild children sat outside the cottage. Cleverer than the bear or the cat, they had opened their cage in the dead of night. Some time after that they had set all the animals free. They spoke no known human language but they had a language of their own.

'We'd better go back to the woods,' said Krall.

'Nothing to keep us here,' agreed Trak.

'If we stay, those other men might find us,' said Krall.

'We don't want that,' said Trak. 'They weren't nice.'

'That old man,' Krall nodded towards the cottage. 'He was nice and the old woman was nice.'

They got up and began to walk away towards the dark and secret forest, in slow satisfaction.

'They weren't just nice,' said Trak. 'They were delicious.' His thin pink tongue came out and licked his thin lips. His eyes blazed. Behind them a ray of sun fell through the open door of the cottage on to the white human bones that lay there on the floor. They gleamed, polished by the gnawing of small, sharp teeth.

Think It Over

Is the story set in England? How can you tell?
   Why had Max been bitten?
How do you know that the children had not been among men and women before?
What did Jorg, the travelling showman, want the children for?
What was the priest's objection to Jorg?
Had Jorg felt sad at the death of the hunchback? How do you know?
What might have happened to the hunchback?
Why did the cat flatten itself against the ground as Jorg passed it?
Why was Jorg's sister, Gisel, cruel to the dog?
What might have made her hiss her words?
How did she feel when she heard Jorg beating the children?
Who was kindest to the animals, Jorg and his sister or the two boys? Give some evidence.
Why did the priest not save the wild children?
Whose bones lay on the floor when the children left? What had happened?

Do You Know?

Can you name a forest in England? In Europe?
What is a forester? What sort of work does he do?
Which bites are dangerous and why?
What society in this country would prosecute for the ill-treatment of animals?
Which wild animal would you fear the most?
How might a man survive alone in a forest? What sort of things in the wild can you eat in safety? What sort of plants and berries are dangerous?
Name any travelling circus you have seen. Have you ever seen a side-show?

What sort of strange things are usually on display?

How do you teach animals to do tricks? What kind of tricks do lions perform? Sea-lions? Performing dogs?

How might the children have opened their cage?

Do you think that Jorg and Gisel got what they deserved? Or were the children evil? Why?

Using Words

'Snapped', 'growled'—these words, which occur in the story, describe the tone of voice in which something is said. Find others which show how words are spoken by the characters in the story and then add two new ones of your own.

The children chattered like monkeys . . .

He ran like the wind . . .

She flies like a bird . . .

Still using the word 'like', rewrite the sentences above making the comparisons more striking and interesting.

'You shut your mouth!' How would you say this to someone, if you wanted to be more polite?

You beat 'em . . . They'll need taming . . . We don't want that . . .

The apostrophe ' shows that certain letters have been missed out. Write out these three sentences in full, putting in the missing letters or words.

An animal that eats other animals of its own kind is a cann. . . .

Someone who does cruel actions for pure pleasure is called a sad. . . .

'Dead of night' What other expressions with 'dead' in them do you know?

'Max looked at the white horse, whose bones stuck through its skin.' Complete these sentences. They need not have anything to do with the story.

'This is the man whose son . . .

'The men were surrounded by dogs whose leader . . .
'My aunty has a house whose windows . . .
'Anything'. How many words beginning with 'any' can you think of? Check the spelling of each as you write it down.

Write Now

With the help of a book identify three things in the countryside that are safe to eat and three that are dangerous. Draw them and write their names with a short description of each.

What happened to the wild children when they got back to the forest? How would they spend the winter? What kind of shelter could they build? Did they live in a cave? Write their story.

Describe Jorg or Gisel more fully, as you imagine them to be.

Have you ever kept an animal as a pet? List five things that ought to be done to take good care of it and five things one should not do.

In play-form write down what happens when Max and the priest find the bones of Jorg and his sister.

Write a poem called 'The Wild Places' or 'Darkness in the Woods'.

Make a list of the best-known wild animals still living in Great Britain.

Which wild animals used to live here and what happened to them?

Council House Ghost

You do not expect a ghost in a council house. Ghosts in castles, yes. Ghosts in stately homes, yes. Ghosts in old inns, yes. But ghosts in council houses, no. Especially when the house was a new one.

But the Jackson family were sure they had a ghost. Mr and Mrs Jackson had just been rehoused. They had lived for many years in an old terraced house that was going to be pulled down. Now they were in a splendid new council house just built on the edge of the city.

It was right from the first night that the knocking began. A persistent knock, knock, knock. Then a pause. And then more knocks. The knocks began about nine and kept up through the night.

+ + + +

'Something wrong with the water system,' said Mr Jackson. 'I must see the foreman tomorrow.'

A plumber came. He put a new valve in the water tank. But that night the knocking was just the same. Another plumber came a week later. He examined the system and recommended a second water tank as the Jacksons had had a shower fitted because Mrs Jackson could not get in a bath. 'The water pressure varies at different times of the day,' he said. 'That'll clear up your trouble.' The tank was installed. The knockings continued.

The Council said there was nothing more they could do. Mr Jackson was angry. He invited a member of the Council to sit in the living room one night. The member of the Council had to admit that the noise was disturbing. He said he was very sorry about Mrs Jackson losing her sleep. He would get a surveyor to look over the house.

The surveyor said it was the plumbing. There must be some badly jointed pipes in the central heating system. They would take the floor up. Indeed this was where the noise seemed to be coming from. It is sometimes hard at first to locate a noise in a house, especially at night. Now Mr Jackson was sure it came from under the floor.

A team of workmen moved in, took up the floor, rejointed the pipes and declared the system perfect.

The knockings continued and this time they came closer together and there was a note of urgency about them. 'It does not sound like a water pipe,' said Mrs Jackson. 'I'm frightened.'

'We'll get to the bottom of it,' said her husband.

'I wish I was back at the Terrace,' she told him.

+ + + +

She certainly did that night, because it was then that the scratching began. 'There's something trying to get into the house,' she said. It sounded like a giant rat, scratching on the concrete of the floor.

'Probably them damn kids,' said Mr Jackson. He went outside. No one was to be seen.

The scratchings and the knockings were now mixed. They went like this: scratch-knock-knock-scratch; scratch-knock-scratch; scratch-scratch; scratch; scratch-scratch-scratch; knock.

'We've got a ghost,' said Mrs Jackson. 'I'm not going to stay in here a moment longer.' Mr Jackson went out with her to ring up a taxi, and she left at once for her daughter's.

+ + + +

But Mr Jackson was not to be beaten. He returned to the room. He sat there for some time and then noticed that there was a pattern to the noises. He had been a scout. He thought the pattern could be morse with the scratch for the dot and knock for the dash. Yes, the word that kept coming out was: P-R-I-E-S-T. His wife was right. They had got a ghost. Something down there was calling for a priest.

He contacted the local council and told them of his theory. The man on the other end of the phone smiled to himself. The floor had already been dug up once, he told Mr Jackson. There was no question of it being dug up again. Why did not Mr Jackson take a holiday? Perhaps when he came back the noises would have stopped.

He returned home. The only thing he could do, apart from dig up the floor himself, was to call in a priest. He was not a religious man but he had read about this kind of thing. He would try anything not to be driven out of his new home.

+ + + +

'Come in, Mr Jackson,' said the Reverend Stack. 'Have I seen you at church?'

'We've only just moved in, sir,' Mr Jackson said, 'and I was wondering if you might help. I must say here and now that I'm not a religious man. But I think I've got a ghost.'

'Where is that?' asked the priest.

'33 Lammas Road.'

'I expect it's the water supply or new timber drying out. Someone else came to see me from the estate the other day. It will clear up.' His voice was slightly shaky and when he looked up Mr Jackson could see that his face was white.

'We've had everything looked at. It's something tapping out a message in morse. It says: priest, priest. That's why I'm here.'

The priest said nothing for a long time. Then he said, 'I do not believe in ghosts. All you can do is pray.' His own hands, held together in a prayer position were shaking. 'Goodnight, Mr Jackson.'

+ + + +

Mr Jackson was very upset. His wife would not return home. He was determined not to move out. The knockings continued. He told a friend about it in the pub where he was now spending his evenings. 'That priest has a duty to help you,' he told him. 'I should contact the Bishop.'

The Bishop was very sympathetic and also very cross. 'I will contact the Reverend Stack at once,' he said. 'He has done an exorcism before. Leave it to me. I will both help and pray for you.'

The Reverend Stack was on his knees praying when the phone rang. With Jackson's visit the haunting memory which he had been trying for months to pray out of his mind had returned. The night he had met his wife's lover on the building site: to discuss their mutual problem, he had said, in a spirit of Christian understanding. He should not have taken the shooting-stick with him. He should not have lost his temper. He should not have battered Simon Lovell to death. He should not have buried the body in the footings of a house; 33 Lammas Road. Ever since he had been trying to convince himself that the killing was just; that the Sixth Commandment did not always apply. Now Jackson had come to him.

+ + + +

The Bishop was angry. 'It is your Christian duty to help this poor man and his wife,' he said.

'Yes, my Lord,' said the Reverend Stack. The wild thought came to him that perhaps this was his way to salvation. If he exorcised the spirit of Lovell, he could be cleansed of the sin. His night was one of torment. The scene with Lovell went over and over in his mind like an action replay.

Trembling, the Reverend Stack was shown into the room. 'I must be alone,' he said. Indeed he must be alone. Was he in his state of sin able to drive out the forces of evil? He was still a priest, he told himself. He clutched a chair. He could run away now and confess to the Bishop. But no, he must try. He must try.

In a stammering voice he began: 'God, the Son of God, who by his death destroyed death, and overcame him with the power of death. Beat down Satan quickly.' He tried to make the sign of the cross. It was as if the air was filled with wet sand; he had to force his fingers through. He breathed very deeply as he did so, gasping and gulping for air while his heart palpitated.

'Deliver this room from all evil spirits, all vain imaginations, projections and phantasms and all deceits of the evil one; and bid them hate no one. Not even me,' he added into the exorcism, 'and my foulness.' His body felt as if it was on the rack, sinews and bones twisted in one great ache and screech of pain. 'But bid depart to the place appointed them, there to remain for ever.' His voice rose to a scream which echoed down the tunnel of his mind.

'God, Incarnate God, who came to give peace, bring peace.'

He then collapsed on his knees and sprinkled the holy water. But as he did so the floor seemed to open up; he had a terrible vision as two bony arms hanging with decomposed flesh reached up for him.

At the inquest the official said it was a gas explosion. That was what had been causing the noises. They had found the vicar's body wrapped round a partly decomposed body, but of whom, a police investigation had failed to find out.

The house was rebuilt but the Jackson's would not live there. Another family, desperate for a house, moved in.

They had no trouble. But the room was always a very cold one despite the central heating. And their pet dog would never enter it.

Think It over

Where had the Jacksons lived previously? What was their new home like?

What was the first sign the ghost made? What did Mr Jackson think it was?

How did the second plumber explain the noises?

How did the surveyor explain them?

Where were the noises coming from?

How did Mrs Jackson feel about it?

What did the noise change into?

What did Mrs Jackson do?

What was strange about the two sorts of sound the ghost made?

What did the man at the Council suggest Mr Jackson should do, when Mr Jackson told him the message?

Was the Reverend Stack eager to come and deal with the ghost? How do you know?

Who did Mr Jackson apply to when he had seen the Reverend Stack?

Why did the Reverend Stack decide at last to go and exorcise the ghost?

What was the official explanation of the vicar's death?

Had the ghost gone after that? How do you know?

Do You Know?

Why do you not expect council houses to be haunted?

Have you ever heard of a council house or flat ghost in your area?

What time was it when the vicar committed the murder? Where is the evidence in the story?

Can you find out from someone what causes knocking in water pipes?

Was the first plumber good at his job?

Why is a water tank put high up in a house?

How do you know that Mrs Jackson is not very well?

Are your floors concrete or wood? Which might be best?

Who invented the Morse code? Is it still used?

Was the crime worse in the vicar's case than for other men? Why?

Who is your local bishop?

Write out one other Commandment from Exodus in the
    Bible.
Have you read any recent cases of exorcism in your local
    paper?
What is holy water?
What is an inquest? When is it held? By whom? Where in
    your town would it be held?
Mr Jackson was in the house. Why might he not have been
    hurt in the accident?
Would you have lived in the rebuilt house? Why?
Do animals have sharper senses than men? Have you any
    evidence of your own?

Using Words

'That'll clear up your trouble.' Use these expressions in
    sentences: clear out; clear off; clear (something) with.
'We'll get to the bottom of it.' Rewrite the sentence without
    using 'get to the bottom of'.
Write out 'priest' in Morse code. Write out your own name
    in the code.
What is the difference between 'exorcise' and 'exercise'?
'Mr Jackson was very upset.' How many other ways can you
    thing of saying this?
Give another word or meaning for 'phantasm'.
'Plumber' has a silent 'b' in it. Complete all the following
    words which have a similar silent 'b':

        d. . . money owed
        c. . . useful for hair
        l. . . you eat it for dinner
        b. . . it explodes
        t. . . you are buried in it
        w. . . you were born in it

Write Now

In play-form. Write the conversation Mr Jackson had with Mrs Jackson after the explosion.

Invent a ghost story which might have happened in your house.

Have you ever wanted to take revenge on someone? If you did, write what happened.

Have you ever moved house? How did you feel? What were your impressions of your new home? What did you have to do to settle in? Write an account.

You are out walking one evening in a lonely wood with your dog. It starts whimpering and refuses to go any further. What happens?

'I do not believe in . . .' Write three things you do not believe in.

Write a poem called 'A Funny Noise in the Night'.

A Night at the Palladium

I was with him at the beginning and at the end. That's how I know. You will only have seen the end. The tragic death on stage of Martin Warlock, lead guitarist of Warlock and the Coven. The Coven? The group? Martin was the Coven. There wasn't a bigger star in Europe—in all the world—at the end.

You probably saw it all on telly. You'd have seen the packed Palladium. They could have sold all the tickets twice over. You'd have seen the stage. You probably wouldn't have noticed the man in the middle of the front row of the audience, though. But I'm going on too fast.

I was with him in the beginning because I was his drummer all along. It wasn't like the Palladium in the beginning. It was Bolton. We used to do gigs like Bolton and Carlisle and Worksop and Kettering and Slough. Up and down the A1 and the M1 and the M6. Always at the bottom of the bill. We had a van. It was held together by chewing gum and string but we owed a packet on it. We still owed a bomb that night for repairs from a month before. But we drove and played, drove and played. We didn't get much sleep. And we didn't make money. It was getting us all down and Martin worst of all. He'd chucked up a good job. We owed a lot on the instruments. The bookings were running out. Like us. We were running, too, and getting nowhere.

+ + + +

Well, there we were in this dressing room in Bolton. Next to the Gents. It was just after one on a Sunday night. February tenth, as a matter of fact. The show was over.

Some herberts had given us the slow handclap. We were all flaked out. We were deep in the clag. Right up the creek without a paddle. We all knew it.

'My God!' Martin started and threw his empty beer can across the room. He'd been drinking during the performance and he'd had a few beers and whisky after we finished. 'If—,' he snarled, 'if—just once—we really made it! Once!'

'Ah! Leave it,' Jack said. He played bass. I forget his second name, now. Gavin, who sang a bit and played piano and organ, said nothing. He never did. We were used to Martin. He'd sound off like that from time to time. He was always a bit wild and more so when he'd had a few drinks. And he was always mad ambitious.

'Come on, Foster, old lad,' I told him. That was Martin's name, then. The 'Warlock' came later when the act got going. 'Let's get it together. We're in West Hartlepool tomorrow night, you know.'

'West Hartlepool!' The way Martin said it, it sounded like another name for Hell.

'Give us a hand, Jack,' I said, 'to get these drums into the van.'

But Martin was still ranting on. 'I'd give my right arm,' he said, 'for a bit of luck. I'd—I'd sell my soul for a chance of success. Anything!'

'Who'd want it?' said Jack. He'd picked up a drum case and opened the door to go out. 'Hello!' he said. There was a man in the corridor outside.

+ + + +

He was a funny looking bloke. He was dark skinned, he had a little black moustache and beard and his eyes had strange, fiery glints in them. He wore black clothes and a long black coat. He came into the room, limping a bit and he never took his hat off the whole time.

We got a few like that—girls, old men who wanted to tell us how wicked we were, young blokes who wanted to join the group, weirdoes and so on. Mostly, as far as we could, we treated them politely. You never know who you're talking to.

'Mr Martin Foster?' he asked.

'That's me,' said Martin. 'What can I do for you?'

'It's what I can do for you, Mr Foster,' the bloke said silkily.

'Oh, yes?' said Martin.

'I watched the act. You deserve better things than you had tonight. I could see that you got it. My organisation is a very old and well-established one. We have never failed to give satisfaction in the past. You are worth success. I can guarantee it.'

'You must be joking,' said Jack.

'Our terms used to be twenty five years,' said the man, ignoring Jack and speaking to Martin. 'Times change, however. The contract period now is for fifteen years. But you will not be disappointed in results. I promise that. Fifteen years. You understand?'

Fifteen years?' Jack said. 'What are you on about?'

'Shut up!' Martin ordered. 'Contract?' he asked.

'Here.' The man pulled it out of one of the wide sleeves of his coat. Martin took it from him. There was an odd expression on his face.

'Hang on, Martin,' I said. 'Morry Smith's still our agent. He won't like this.'

'Shut up!' Martin said again.

'Mr Smith won't mind at all. I assure you.' The man smiled at me. It sent chills up my spine. He seemed to have an odd factory kind of smell about him for one thing. For another—he seemed to give off heat like a radiator. He was still wearing that old-fashioned looking hat.

+ + + +

'I'll sign,' Martin said. 'Success? You guarantee it, if I sign?'

'Definitely.'

'A pen.' Martin clicked his fingers impatiently.

'Hang on, Martin,' I objected again. 'Read what it says first, at least.'

'I know what it will say,' Martin whispered. He looked suddenly pale and grim. 'Give me a pen.'

'Use this.' From nowhere the man produced an old-fashioned pen with a steel nib.

'And the ink?' said Martin as if he already knew the answer.

'Use a drop of blood.'

'Strewth!' Jack burst out. 'You are a right weirdo, mate. Martin! What's going on?'

But it was no use. Martin had stuck the pen into his hand. We were too astonished to say a word. Besides, the man scared us. We all stared at the bright drop of blood on Martin's palm. The only sound in the silence was the scratching as he signed his name.

+ + + +

Well, you probably know the rest of it. There was the tour of America, the world tour, the villa in the South of France, the recording contracts, the Rolls, the films. You'll know about Nel Troyes, too, Martin's wife. She was said to be the most beautiful woman in the world. Oh yes, Martin had everything along the way.

Until that night at the Palladium. You would have seen Martin collapse and the curtain come down. The compere announced that he had had a slight accident and that the show would continue in a few minutes. The following day the newspapers said heart failure. I have my doubts.

The show had started later than usual. We had a sort of black magic effect in a number that Martin wanted to put on exactly at midnight. So it was about one o'clock when it happened. Martin stopped playing suddenly. The group's playing came to a ragged halt. I saw Martin staring down into the audience. He looked as though he was seeing something deeper than the floor. Deeper than the grave.

Then he dropped his guitar and made a sweep with his arms. He was like a man shielding his body from the flames. His scream as he fell was the most horrible thing I have ever heard.

+ + + +

Things went crazy for a while on stage. In front of the curtain the compere managed to keep the audience quiet and amused. Behind it there was panic. Someone did ring for an ambulance. I was standing back from Martin's body. From somewhere they'd managed to get a doctor to look at him.

'Was he shot?' a voice behind me asked.

'Shot? No.' I turned round. 'Why?' It was one of the programme sellers who had asked. She must have made her way at once on to the stage.

'There was this man,' she said. 'When he—when Warlock fell on the stage, this man got to his feet. He clapped his hands slowly together, like someone catching a butterfly. Then he just walked straight out of the theatre.'

'Martin wasn't shot,' I said. 'He just—went. What did this man look like?'

'He gave me the shivers,' she said. 'He was all in black. He had a little beard and a moustache. He limped a bit as he went out. I'd swear, too, that he was wearing a wig. It was as though he had something on his head that he wanted to hide. He went right past me. I could see his smile and his eyes. They were red.'

'Red?' I remembered even then that night in Bolton.

'I was as close to him as I am to you,' she went on. 'When he went past me, it was as if someone had opened an oven. And he had a smell about him. Sulphur.' She looked at Martin. 'He's dead, isn't he?' She began to cry.

The cause of death was confirmed as heart failure. You may have seen the funeral on the news on telly. The papers talked about the stresses on a pop star, the strain on the heart. But no one saw anything strange about Martin's death. Tragic, yes. But not strange. So I haven't said anything. The programme seller hasn't talked about it either. Not to my knowledge. But I did work it out. The show at the Palladium took place on February the tenth. It was exactly fifteen years to the day and to the hour from that moment in the dressing room in Bolton. I don't really know what to think about it. But for those fifteen years Martin had all the luck in the world. You could say that he had the luck of the devil.

Think It Over

Why would many people have witnessed Martin Warlock's death?

What would they probably not have noticed?

What is the real beginning to the story?

Why were the group depressed?

What was Martin's ambition? What had increased his angry mood?

What does he say that might give you a hint about what happens?

How did the man outside know what was going on in the dressing room? Was he just listening? Can you think of another reason after reading the story?

Why might the stranger have kept his hat on?

What suggests that Martin might know who the stranger is?

What two clues are given the reader about the stranger's identity?

How did the stranger fulfil his part of the bargain? How famous did the Coven become?

What might Martin have seen as he stared down into the audience?

Why might the man have clapped his hands together as if catching a butterfly?

What does the teller of the tale believe was the cause of Martin's death? Why did Martin die fifteen years after signing the contract?

Do You Know?

What is a warlock? What is a coven? What might 'Warlock and the Coven' suggest about the kind of effects the group uses and the music they play?

Which is the most attractive town you have been in? Which is the most depressing? Compare your answers with others in the class. Is there any disagreement? What makes a town either attractive or depressing?

What is the difference between an A road and an M road? Are there any C roads?

How much money would you need to get the equipment for a group?

How many guitarists are there in your favourite pop group? Which, in the opinion of your class, was the most popular group a year ago? Which is the most popular group now? Name any well-known group that had a hard time in getting to the top.

Where is the Palladium? How would you find out what is on there this week?

Find on a map the towns mentioned in paragraph three. Which two are the farthest apart?

What did the stranger mean by 'my organisation'? Why did he not give it its proper name?

What does the Devil usually offer in exchange for a person's soul? Was there anything unusual about the agreement Martin made?

Why does the Devil smell of sulphur?

What does an agent do? What is a contract?

What do you do when you are impatient?

What would you like to be a success at and why?

Do you think Martin was happy with his riches? Why?

Why would the group's black magic number be done at midnight?

How do you think the audience might have reacted to Martin's collapse?

Using Words

A 'gig' is a word used mainly by musicians. What does it mean?

Write the following in more everyday English: 'We still owed a bomb', 'Some herberts', 'All flaked out', 'deep in the clag', 'up the creek without a paddle'.

'I'd give my right arm . . .' What other expressions do you know which are based on parts of the body? Try using these: foot, teeth, neck, nose.

What expressions do you know with 'luck' or 'unlucky' in them?

What is the difference between 'getting it together' and 'getting it over with'?

How would you define a 'weirdo'? Compare your definition with that of others. Is there complete agreement in the class about what a weirdo is? If not, why not?

What does 'rant' mean?

Name some of the differences between the way the Devil speaks and the way in which members of the group and the teller of the tale speak.

'The group's playing came to a ragged halt.' What does the word 'ragged' tell you about the way the music stopped?

In these words 'ei' does not follow a 'c': neither, either, their, weird, neighbour, weight, height. Learn them.

Give another title to the story.

Write Now

Make a list of the people who work in a theatre.

Write a poem called 'The Flames of Hell' or 'Watching a Group'.

In play-form write out the conversation the programme seller had with her family when she got home.

Write the story of a black magician and what happens when

he tries to gain power by summoning evil spirits.

Write a newspaper account of Martin's death. Give your work a headline.

The story teller and the drummer discuss Martin's death and what the group will do after it. Write it in play-form.

List a number of groups using special effects, stating what kind of effects they use.

Vampires

Mark Ogden was just dropping off when he heard the leathery flapping in the pine trees. It brought him out of his sleeping bag. He knelt in the tent doorway and looked around. When he looked up he seemed to see something large and black cutting off the moon for a moment. A bat?

The flapping stopped. He got out of the tent and put his boots on. He would take a look round. Maybe someone was having a joke with him. Maybe, in this wild, faraway corner of Europe, they did not like strangers. Not many tourists ever came as far as this. It was the loneliest of places. Walking all day, he had met no one. But that was why he had chosen the place for a holiday. He had camped in remote spots, he had been on his own before. He shivered suddenly. He had never felt like this.

Across the clearing something rustled. He peered into the darkness. Then the man stepped out from the blackness of the trees and Ogden gasped.

+ + + +

He was tall and thin; a long, black cloak fell from his shoulders. His face shone bone white in the moonlight.

'Wait!' Ogden called. 'Who are you?' Now, as the stranger slowly advanced, he could see the white shirt front, the black gloves on the raised hands. He could not see the face clearly but he could see the smile. That gleamed horribly. Most horrible of all were the eyes. They seemed to glimmer with a light of their own. They were like rubies, blood-red. An ancient terror woke in Ogden. He screamed and ran.

+ + + +

54

It was a chase that lasted the rest of the night. Whenever he stopped he heard the crackling in the woods behind him, coming slowly on. Once, where the woodland grew thin, when he paused, he heard flapping above him and plunged on, sobbing with fear.

The moon had gone and the sky was bright with dawn when he saw the big house. He ran up the long, grass-grown driveway and hammered on the door. No one came. He twisted the door handle and the door opened. He went in, slammed it behind him and leaned against it, breathing hard.

+ + + +

It was semi-dark in the hall. He called out but no one answered. He called again. Then he saw a light glimmering. It came towards him and he saw that it was a candle carried by a girl. She wore a long white gown and her feet were bare. Long black hair fell on her shoulders. She was pale. Her face was thin. She looked thin and weak. But she was still beautiful.

'I'm sorry,' he gasped. 'Bursting in like this. I was chased. There's something out there.' He pointed a trembling finger. 'It was after me. Its eyes—'

'Don't worry,' she said. Her voice, too, was weak, almost a whisper. She turned her head and called softly, 'Father!'

A man came along the corridor that led to the back of the house. Ogden stepped forward, offering his hand. 'My name's Ogden,' he said. 'I made camp very late. Out there in the woods. Then I saw something. I ran. I've been running—I don't know how long.'

'You have been lucky,' the man told him. 'I am Jaroslav Breska. This is my daughter Elena. We know well what has frightened you. You are very welcome here.' He shook Ogden's hand. His grip was cold and without strength. 'Come this way. You must be very tired.'

+ + + +

Breska and Elena escorted Ogden up the wide staircase.

Both father and daughter moved slowly as if they were ill. Ogden was shown into a large bedroom.

'Sleep,' Breska advised. He indicated the canopied bed. 'We can talk later. Now it is morning, you are safe.'

Ogden slept deeply and dreamlessly. When he woke, the room was still dark, shaded by thick curtains. Elena was standing by his bed, holding a tray. He sat up, remembering, puzzled.

'You and your father—you speak English?'

'Oh, yes. In our time we have learned many languages. Here is soup. Drink it and then you can sleep again. My father will come and talk to you when you are rested.'

'What was the thing I saw?'

'My father will explain. Have the soup now.' He did as she told him. When he had finished it, he could hardly keep his eyes open. He lay back and slept again.

+ + + +

When he awoke, Breska was sitting by the bed.

'You seem better,' he said mildly.

'Yes. I'm fine. But—what was that thing? Was it really there at all?' The light in the room came from a candle. The curtains were still drawn. Breska's face was dim.

'An unhappy creature,' Breska said. 'We call them vampires.'

Ogden had no desire to laugh. He had known it all along. But he had not dared to admit it to himself. Memories of what he had read came back to him. He felt cold.

'How long have I slept?' he asked.

'All day. It is nearly night.'

'I'd better get back and see to my things. My camp——'

'No. It would be dangerous. You must stay here.'

Ogden's eyes stared at the semi-darkness of the room. Vampires. It was like a disease. The victim of a vampire became a vampire himself. Then, if he, too, drank living human blood, he could never die. But he was cut off from normal humanity for ever. He became sensitive to light.

Direct sunlight was torture to him. Too much of it could destroy him. Mankind defended itself against such creatures. Garlic over windows and doors was a sure shield. So was a cross. It was an evil fate to be a vampire. Without a diet of fresh human blood, the vampire grew weak, though it could not die. It had to wait, shrouded from the light, until, like a fly to a spider's web, its prey came along.

'That's what saved me,' he exclaimed.

'What?'

'That thing—the vampire—it had been starved too long. It was too weak to attack while I could defend myself. Then daylight was coming—'

'Perhaps,' said Breska. 'But darkness is not far off now. You must not leave this house to wander in the forest.'

'No.' Ogden shivered suddenly. 'Thank you for letting me stay.'

'We are pleased to have you,' Breska told him. 'Rest again now. Drink your wine. You must stay here. It will soon be time for us to dine. Elena and I will come to you when it is time.' He put the glass of wine on the table and left the room.

+ + + +

But it tasted bitter. Ogden was strangely uneasy and restless. He got up and walked across to the curtains. When he drew them back, he saw how dark it had grown. Beyond the untidy hedge that surrounded the garden, he could see the woods dense and threatening. The garden was very overgrown. When he pulled the curtains right back, there was still enough light in the sky for him to see the room more clearly. Everything in it looked old. Old and dusty. The bedclothes were yellow with age.

He went along the landing and looked at the other rooms. All the other rooms were curtained, too. By the light of the candle he carried, he could see how unused they, too, looked.

Something drew him downstairs. The rooms he looked

into down there were heavily curtained and dark. At the end of the corridor on the ground floor was a door that led down steps to a cellar. Ogden did not go down. The cellar smelled of earth, of graves.

+ + + +

He could hear no sound in the house. He walked slowly back along the corridor and called out.

'In here, Mr Ogden.' It was Elena's voice. It was no longer weak and faint. It was full and sweet. He could not help himself. He went into the room at the front of the house.

Two candles burned there, making the shadows dance. Elena was there and so was Breska. But they had changed. Their cheeks were flushed; their eyes were bright and red. With a sweep of his arm, Breska threw back the curtains. It was now fully dark outside.

'Night time,' said Breska, smiling a bright, fanged smile. 'Now we come into our own. At night we have our full strength.'

+ + + +

Ogden had no power to run. His stumbling steps carried him towards them. Breska seized his arm in his black-gloved hand. The fingers were no longer weak. They held him fast.

Elena's beautiful face bent towards him. She panted slightly. He felt her full, red lips on his neck. His terror was so great that he could not scream. As her teeth entered his neck, he felt little pain. Strength flowed out of him and he fainted.

When he recovered, all fear had left him. He was filled with a strange and terrible joy. Breska was bending over him and the old man nodded.

'Come,' he said. He and Elena led the way out of the room and out of the front door. Ogden got to his feet and followed eagerly. Now, he knew only one thing. He was thirsty.

Think It Over

What made Mark Ogden think of bats?

How do you know that he usually enjoys being in lonely places?

What was the most horrible thing about the stranger in the cloak and why?

What might have told Ogden that the house did not have many visitors?

What struck him about both the father and the daughter?

Why did he not know what time of day it was when he first woke?

Do you think there was anything strange about the soup he was given? What might have been in it?

What was odd about the room when he awoke the second time?

Why were all the curtains always drawn in the house?

What sort of things made Ogden begin to be suspicious?

Why had Breska and his daughter waited until night time?

What happened to Ogden in the end?

Do You Know?

How much does a sleeping bag cost?

Which country might Ogden have been in?

Why do some people like to be alone?

Do you think that Breska was the man Mark Ogden first saw in the clearing? Why?

Who wrote a famous book about vampires? What is the book called? What is the name of the vampire in it? From what country did he come? What are supposed to be the marks of a vampire?

What are the most fearsome eyes you have seen?

When Ogden first came into the house was the girl's reaction to him a normal one? How might she have reacted to him?

What makes a person's hands tremble? Is it only fear or can there be other causes?

What sort of people have cold hands on a warm day? Why are their hands cold?

In former times beds had canopies over them and curtains to draw round them. Do you know why? Can you guess? Or find out?

Apart from making a room private, what other reasons are there for having curtains at a window?

Why are the vampires in the story not so weak at night?

Why might garlic be hung at doors and windows to keep vampires away?

Explain the end of the story.

Using Words

Make up a sentence, using 'dropping off' in another sense from that in the story.

'Bone white'. Give three other words to describe white.

'You must be very tired.' What other ways are there of saying this?

Complete these comparisons: The cat's eyes were like . . .; the monster's eyes were like . . .; the old lady's eyes were like . . .

'Wait!' Ogden called. 'Who are you?' Write a short dialogue which need not have anything to do with the story, in which the exclamation mark (!) and the question mark (?) are used correctly.

'He ran up the long grass-grown driveway and hammered on the door.' Which word shows that he was frightened and in a hurry? What word would you have used to show that he was calling at the house in an ordinary way?

'Shrouded from the light' What is a shroud?

Do you have a 'landing' in your house? What is it? Name all the rooms in your house. Have all the class given similar names for each room? Account for any differences.

'Rest again now. Drink your wine.' These are commands. How many commands can you think of that appear round us on notices and in advertisements?

'Terror' All the following words end in -or. Complete them. (You look into it) m . . ., (He treats you when ill) d . . ., (He or she wins) v . . ., (He is in a play) a . . ., (It joins up rooms) c . . . .

Write Now

You are chased by a wild animal. Describe the experience in a short paragraph.

Describe in a few sentences the feelings you have when you have been running hard.

In a short paragraph, describe a sinister house at the end of a long driveway. You might use these words: ivy, shutters, blinds, crumbling, creaking, pale face at a window.

Write the story of what happened when Ogden went out that night with Breska and Elena.

Write in play-form the conversation that might go on at the local inn about the old house.

Rewrite the end of the story, enabling Mark Ogden to escape.

A friend of yours falls ill and stays all day in his darkened bedroom. On a visit you notice that his teeth seem to have grown rather long. What happens?

Gargoyle

He had to have the chalice. With the power he already had, he had looked into the future. He would sit in a high place. Nothing could harm him. He would live forever. But he needed the power of the chalice. Alex Morland had advanced through all the degrees of magic. There had been at first the small group. A girl had committed suicide for his sake. There had been other sacrifices. He had advanced through the ceremonies of blood, the rites at midnight in the ruined church. Now he had left them all behind. He did not need the group any longer. By himself he was strong enough. But, for the last step, he had to have the chalice. And it was there for him to take in Moldgrave Church.

+ + + +

No one would have known that Alex Morland was a black magician. There was nothing in the way he dressed, nothing in the way he spoke, to give him away. Only his eyes, in a certain light, suggested the power of evil that was in him. The verger in Moldgrave Church had no suspicions.

He showed Morland round the church, talking of its history. The Abbot's Chalice was made of gold. It stood in a glass case near the altar.

'Is it safe here?' Morland asked. 'Aren't you afraid someone will steal it?'

'No.' The verger shook his head. 'It's protected by an alarm.' Morland took careful note of the wire that ran up to the case. 'Besides,' the verger went on, 'there's a legend about it. That protects it, too. It's been in this church a long time.'

'The Abbot?' Morland turned his head away to hide a sneer.

'The Abbot—or something,' the verger agreed solemnly. 'There have been one or two attempts to steal the chalice during the past hundred years. They came to nothing. The chalice always returned.'

+ + + +

Then the Vicar appeared. A talkative man, he was glad to see Morland. Morland repeated his tale about writing a book and the Vicar accompanied them round the church. When they had finished, he followed Morland outside, still talking.

'There's something else out here,' he said. 'It might give you another interesting little tale for this book of yours. Look!' He pointed up at the roof. 'See that gargoyle, that stone figure up there?'

Morland looked up. The sun was bright on it. The figure, half-devil, half-human, crouched at the edge of the roof.

'What about it?' he asked.

'That is the Black Abbot of Moldgrave. He gave the chalice you have just seen to the church.'

'He doesn't look like an abbot to me,' Morland grunted scornfully.

'Oh—it isn't a figure, a carving of the abbot. But it's an interesting little story. Let me tell you about it.'

'Must you?' growled Morland. But the Vicar did not hear him.

'A wicked man,' the Vicar explained. 'He lived in the fourteenth century.' He went on to tell Morland how the Abbot had lived a life of pleasure, womanising, drinking, hunting, neglecting his duties, ignoring God. Just before he died, however, either through fear or true repentance, he had changed. He had spent some of his enormous wealth on the golden chalice and given it to the church. It had escaped the clutches of Henry VIII and of Cromwell's men and, as Morland had seen, the Church still possessed it.

'The legend has it,' the Vicar continued chattily, 'that the chalice saved the Abbot from Hell. But he didn't get away with it. He didn't go to Heaven, either. He stayed here on earth. Not as a man—but as a gargoyle. That stone figure—' he pointed again, 'imprisons the soul of the Abbot. He must stay there until doomsday, or until a wickedness is found to match his own. That's how the old chronicle puts it.'

'Does it?' said Morland. He hardly bothered to be polite. He had plans to make and wanted to get away. 'An amusing story, Vicar. Good morning.'

+ + + +

It was not difficult to steal the chalice. Morland went into the church the next evening and hid in the robing room. The verger locked up and left the church in darkness. Morland came out, cut the wire of the alarm, cut the glass of the case and stole the chalice. Picking the lock of the church from the inside was not difficult, either. The only danger was in being spotted as he came out. But the churchyard was empty and so was the road outside. No one saw him on the way back to his hotel.

It was part of his plan to stay in Moldgrave for a day or two. If he left immediately after the theft of the chalice, he might draw attention to himself. He would lie low. If he sensed that the police suspected him, then would be the time to disappear.

But the police took in a local man, Beech, for questioning. He was slightly unbalanced and had been tried before for damaging church property. Then, Morland decided to leave on the following day.

+ + + +

That night he was strangely tired. He went early to bed and fell asleep almost immediately. He did not know how long he had been asleep before the dream came.

A voice called him. It was an old man's thin, cracked and evil. He could not refuse. He got up, took the chalice from its hiding place and went downstairs and out into the street. Weird clouds were chasing across the sky. Then he was in the churchyard.

He awoke. It had not been a dream. The place was full of a nightmare glow. But it was real. He was not asleep. His throat was too dry with fear to call out. There were voices around him, whispering and chattering. Shadowy shapes slithered among the gravestones.

And the dreadful figure coming down the side of the church was real, too. For a moment he thought that it was a man. But it was too small and squat; its steps were too slow and heavy. It was the gargoyle.

+ + + +

When it was almost on him, he could see its face. There was no mouth, the nose was broken away. But its eyes were alive with an eager joy. He could neither scream nor run.

The thing did not crush him but seemed to flow over him like water. At the last moment, as it swallowed him up, he was able to give a yell of terror. But his cry was lost in a louder sound. Something escaped from the gargoyle as he became its prisoner. It shouted in triumph. The Black Abbot of Moldgrave was free, after centuries of imprisonment. But Alex Morland was not.

+ + + +

The chalice was found in the churchyard the following day. The mystery of its disappearance was never cleared up. No one connected Morland with it. The manager of the hotel kept Morland's luggage. After some months, when he had heard nothing from Morland, he sold the luggage to pay the hotel bill.

The vicar still tells the tale of the Abbot's soul imprisoned in the gargoyle. There is no reason, obviously, for anyone to think otherwise.

Only—last autumn—one of the workmen cleaning the stonework of the church had a bit of a fright. He cried out and his mate came along the scaffolding towards him.

'What's up, Bert?' he asked.

'That thing!' Bert gasped and pointed to the gargoyle. 'Just for a second—It gave me the creeps. Its eyes—! They seemed to be alive.'

'It's getting dusk,' his mate said. 'A trick of the light.'

'Maybe,' said Bert. But he would not go back up on the scaffolding again. Not, he said, if it cost him his job.

It was a good many days before the memory of it stopped coming back to him. For a moment, the eyes of the gargoyle had been alight with the power of evil. They had had horror and rage in them, too. They had looked like the eyes of a trapped thing. Trapped until doomsday.

Think It Over

Why did Alex Morland want the chalice?

What had helped him to become a black magician?

What was there about him that suggested that he was an evil man?

Why were the authorities not afraid of the chalice being stolen? There are two reasons.

Who had given the chalice to the church?

Why had he not gone to heaven?

Whereabouts in the church did Alex Morland hide?

How did he prevent the alarm going off?

Why did he stay in Moldgrave after that?

Who was arrested for the theft of the chalice? Why?

When did Morland find out that he was not dreaming? What was strange about the churchyard?

Whose soul is now in the gargoyle? How long will it be trapped there?

Do You Know?

What is a Black Mass? Where, according to report, is it held?

What is supposedly the usual dress for a magician?

Name two abbeys in England. Do monks still live there? What kind of a monk is an abbot?

Do people's eyes reveal their character? Discuss.

What is a gargoyle? Are there any on a church or cathedral near you? Why are they put on churches?

Give the date of the first year of the fourteenth century and the last. Explain why this century is called the twentieth.

What is doomsday? Why is it so called?

Why are churches full of old objects? What is a chalice? What is the robing room in a church? What does a verger do? What was an altar originally used for?

Name a statue or legendary being which is half man and half animal.

What is an old chronicle?

How do you clean stonework? Have you ever watched anyone doing it? Can you find out?

Can you name any other stories in which a man or a woman is turned into another being?

Using Words

'Gargoyle' is a peculiar word. If you know what it does, can you guess the connection between it and the word 'gargle'?

'He would sit in a high place.' Look at paragraph one and say what you think the sentence means.

Write out in words all the numbers from tenth to nineteenth.

'Enormous' List all the words you can think of meaning 'big'.

'He would lie low.' What single word means 'lie low'?

'Shadowy shapes slithered.' Make up two sentences in which many of the words begin with the same letter to describe (a) something pleasant, and (b) something unpleasant.

A man who walks in his sleep is called a somna. . . .

'It gave me the creeps.' How many other ways can you think of saying this?

How many words can you find in the story that relate specifically to a church?

-owe -uff -ow -oo -off. Write out each of these sounds at the head of five columns. 'Enough' goes in the -uff column. Now put each of the following words into its correct column: rough, dough, bough, through, cough, tough.

Make a list of all the words in the story that end in -ly and learn their spelling.

Write Now

Write your own story about a spirit imprisoned in a cave or a stone or a tree. Does it get out? How? What happens?

Describe in a few sentences a really evil face.

Make up your own legend about some place or building or object in your area. *OR*, find out some legend about a church or famous house near you and write an account.

Describe a churchyard.

Write a poem called, 'The Eyes of Stone' or 'The Talkative Man'.

Write a short piece in which you see things slithering and sliding all round you. It could be about a dream or another planet.

In play-form. Bert tells his family about his experience on the roof of the church. His wife thinks he has been dreaming.

Mirrors

Dear George,

Write to me when you have read this. Tell me it's all non-sense. Don't be afraid, Tell me I'm crazy. That will be a relief.

It began normally enough. The Ruffton Playhouse is near my surgery. You will remember the place. We saw 'Night Must Fall' there together some years ago.

He was an actor. He had seen my brass plate on the way to the theatre and so he telephoned for an appointment. He was a man of about thirty and he was called Neil Baxter. He was pleasant and sensible and seemed a very steady sort of man. He wanted a thorough examination. He said that his eyes had been bothering him.

Well, I gave him the usual tests. I examined and tested his eyes. There was nothing wrong with them. There was nothing wrong with him, either. When he came for the results and I told him, I was surprised. He seemed disappointed. Depressed. He wanted to talk.

'Doctor,' he said. 'If people are—well—if they're not right in the head—can you tell?'

+ + + +

'I think so,' I told him. 'I might have to see them once or twice.'

'How do you tell?'

'By the way they talk,' I said. 'By the way they act.'

'Am I?'

'No,' I said. 'I'm pretty sure of that.' I thought perhaps he was a bit nervous. He seemed, as I said, a very steady sort of man. Maybe he had not been sleeping well. I was going to give him some tablets.

'Do they see things?' he asked.

'Some do. Sometimes,' I said. 'Why?'

'I see things,' he said.

'When you're tired? Have you had some trouble with your eyes before? When do you see things?'

'I only see them in one place,' he said. 'I'm an actor, as you know. I sit in front of a mirror in my dressing room to make myself up. I see things in the mirror. Odd things. They are not in the room behind me.'

I thought, then, that he was worrying about nothing. I had other patients waiting. Actors get strung up before they go on stage. Our eyes play tricks on us all at times. I gave him some tablets and told him to come back the following week. If there was really anything wrong, I could send him to a specialist.

When he came back, he was just the same. Quiet. Steady. But very worried. He was still seeing things in the mirror. But they were clearer now. I examined his eyes again and did other tests. His eyes were fine. There was nothing physically wrong that I could see. But it was beginning to look like a case for a specialist. And perhaps not just an eye specialist. Perhaps he did need a specialist for the mind. I gave him some different tablets. I told him to see how things went. I asked him to come again in a week. And then some strange things started to happen.

+ + + +

I was having my hair cut a day or two later. The barber was snipping away and talking. Suddenly he stopped dead. He moved away from my chair and went up to the mirror which hung facing me. He muttered something to himself and brushed the surface of the mirror with his fingers. Then he stared all round the shop. He looked quite scared. He frowned into the mirror again for a moment. Then he shook his head and went back to cutting my hair. I asked him what the matter was but he said it was nothing. After that he hardly talked at all.

When Baxter came again, he was different. He seemed more excited. I began to be worried about him. And yet—he told it all so calmly—so sensibly.

+ + + +

It had started about a fortnight before he came to see me. One evening he had looked into the mirror and had been startled. Something, a flicker, a cloud, had come and gone in the room behind him. He had thought little of it. Then it had happened again. And again. The cloud, the flicker had taken shape. It had stayed longer. And longer.

It was like this now. He would look into the mirror and it would change. It was like looking into a window. He could still see his own face but it was dim and ghostly. On the glass he could still vaguely see the room. Sometimes he turned away from the mirror and looked. There was his dressing room behind him, sharp and clear. Empty. Normal. But when he looked back at the mirror, he saw a different place. It was hard to describe. It did not seem to be in this world.

And the cloudiness and flickering had taken shape. He could see them almost clearly now. Not men. Not insects. They had heads that seemed to be melting. Their faces were pointed. Or, perhaps, they had beaks. They were dark in colour, tall, with long arms or feelers. They had long thin hands or claws. They whispered together. At times they looked to be pointing. At him.

Then they would fade as quickly as they came. There would only be the familiar dressing room in the mirror. And his own face, staring back at himself. Pale and haunted.

I told him he needed a rest, a holiday. I would fix it up for him to see another doctor. He said he would take a holiday but he had another ten days to work. He couldn't let the theatre down.

The next day I was in the older part of town. I had to pay a visit to an old lady who is one of my patients. She kept me talking. When I left her, I found I had only about half an hour for lunch. I slipped into a pub.

There were two men there in white overalls. One of them was talking about his wife. He sounded more amused than upset. Apparently she had taken down all the mirrors in their house. She said that she saw things in the mirror and they scared her. The husband seemed to think it was quite funny. He said that women were like that and she would soon get over it.

That night Baxter came to my house. I didn't expect him. It was quite late but I let him in. He talked a lot. It was all about a theory he had. It concerned these things that he had seen in the mirror. I was really worried about him. It was late before I got him to go. I told him to go straight to bed and sleep as long as he could. It seemed to me that he ought not to go near that dressing room again. He ought to stop looking in mirrors, too. I told him that. But he said that it was only another week. He could not let his friends at the theatre down.

That's nearly the end of it, George. What does it sound like? I'm imagining things, aren't I? Baxter's story is affecting me. He was obviously heading for a breakdown. But there are just one or two more things before I end this.

+ + + +

Baxter died during the week. They found him in his dressing room. In front of that damned mirror. Old Noble, the doctor who examined him, told me that there was no obvious reason for the death. His heart had just stopped. Noble talked about the expression on Baxter's face. He said that it looked as though Baxter had died of fright.

That was bad enough. It upset me. I felt guilty about it. Perhaps I could have done more for poor Baxter. But it's that theory of Baxter's which I can't get off my mind. It's mad; it's crazy. But I thought about it all yesterday. It's the reason why I'm writing to you now.

That night Baxter came to my house he talked about

other worlds. He might have meant other planets; he might have meant something else. He talked about strange beings, evil creatures, demons. They planned to invade this world. But they would need a gateway. They would need many gateways. Then, all at the same time, they could come through in their thousands—their millions—and kill.

Every house, probably every native hut, has some kind of mirror in it. According to Baxter, that was the way they would come. Through the mirrors, They were there already; watching and waiting for the right moment.

He knew; he had seen them. Other people had probably seen them, too. But what was the use of that? Maybe these strange creatures, these demons were clever enough to know. You can't tell anybody about a theory like that. Your friends wouldn't believe you. A world behind mirrors? They would think you were joking—or mad.

That's why I'm writing to you, George. I've known you a long time. I can trust you. I know you'll give me a straight answer. I can't talk to anyone else about this. The fact is that I believe Baxter.

He told me, too, about a vision he had. Soon, while half the world is asleep, they'll come stalking through the mirrors. Whispering together, their claws clicking, their beaks ready to strike and tear. Only a few of us will expect them. But we'll be too terrified even to scream.

You notice I say, 'us' George. That's it. Tell me it's mad to think like that. I shan't mind.

You see, this morning again, while I was shaving, I saw the cloudiness, the flicker in the mirror. It wasn't a reflection of anything in the bathroom behind me. I saw it yesterday, too. Today, it lasted an instant or two longer.

So, write to me, George. Or—better still—phone.

Yours,

Martin

Think It Over

How soon do you know that it is a doctor writing the letter?

How old was Neil Baxter? How did the doctor feel about him at first?

What was Baxter worrying about?

Where did he see the things that frightened him?

What was there about his room that made him think his eyes were playing tricks?

What did the doctor think was the cause of Baxter's nervousness at first?

What was the result of all the physical tests?

Who was another person to see the strange things? How did the doctor know about it?

What did the things look like when Baxter first saw them? What did they look like later?

Why did Baxter not take a holiday?

Who else, then, talked about the strange sights?

What happened to Baxter in the end?

Who were the things in the mirror? What was Baxter's theory? Why were they there?

Why is the doctor writing the letter?

Do You Know?

What kinds of people advertise their profession by a name plate outside their offices?

What would 'Night Must Fall' be?

Who would you normally see to have your sight tested?

What kind of man would you expect an actor to be?

What can be unlucky about mirrors? Why do some people cover mirrors in a storm? What is the famous story about the girl who went through a mirror into a country beyond it?

Have you ever looked into a distorting mirror at a fair?

What did you look like?

Some people say they have seen UFOs. What do the letters mean? Can you think of a way in which their sight might have deceived them?

If we were invaded from outer space how, do you think, would it happen?

Why does an actor need to make himself up before he goes on stage?

What is missing from the top of this particular letter?

What sort of workmen wear white overalls? List the people whose job you can tell from the way they dress.   ,

Had Baxter died of fright? What other reasons might there have been?

How important is it to have someone you can talk to about your problems? Is there someone in your family? Have you a friend who will listen without laughing at or criticising you? What would you have done in the doctor's case? Written a letter? Told someone?

Using Words

Punctuate the following: 'do they see things he asked some do sometimes I said why I see things he said when you're tired have you had some trouble with your eyes before when do you see things'. Don't forget the question marks. When you have done it, check your version with the story.

A doctor who deals with disturbed minds is called a psych. . . .

What is the difference between, 'She made herself up' and 'She made the story up'? Use 'He could not make it out . . .' and 'The dog made off with . . .' in sentences of your own.

'Actors get strung up.' How many other ways can you think of saying 'strung up'? 'It's all nonsense.' How many other ways are there of saying this?

How many words connected with the medical profession
can you find in the story?

Use 'slipped' in these three different ways in three sentences
of your own: slipped up, slipped into, slipped by.

How many words can you think of in which the letters 'ie'
occur? Check with the dictionary to make sure you have
all of them right.

Write Now

Draw what you think Baxter saw in the mirror.

Write a plan for a TV play called 'Evil Invasion'.

You are looking into a mirror when suddenly you see a
strange face there. Continue the story from there.

Write a letter to a friend asking for some help or advice
about a problem.

In play-form write the conversation the barber might have
with his wife when he got home, OR write the conversation when George tells his wife about Martin's strange
letter.

Quake

Mr Otis Cornblower was tending his roses one day when he pricked his finger. He did not like the sight of blood and he sat down, as he had become slightly dizzy. As he sat, the earth in the rose bed seemed to erupt before him and the blue of the sky became a great wave. Clouds of dust seemed to sweep up in the whirl of a tornado. He then saw blocks of flats crumbling, cars being crushed, trees falling and water rushing through subways.

The vision then disappeared and he sat in the calm peace of his rose garden wondering what had happened to him. And then a date kept going through his mind: Friday the 13th of January; Friday the 13th of January; Friday the 13th of January.

Mr Cornblower lived alone. He had no one to talk to about his experience. He went inside for a cup of coffee. His pulse was racing. Nothing like this had ever happened to him before. He rarely day-dreamed. He thought he had better see a doctor for a check-up.

+ + + +

The doctor examined him after hearing the story which Mr Cornblower had great embarrassment at telling. 'You are quite physically fit, though a little overweight,' he said. 'But I think that mentally you are under a slight strain. Nothing much. Just a touch of anxiety. Not enough to see a psychiatrist.' He laughed to allay Mr Cornblower's fears. 'Very common. I'll just give you some tablets. Come and see me in a month to see how you're getting on.'

Mr Cornblower felt better after seeing the doctor. He thought he would go for a walk in the park before going to bed. But as he stepped in the park he had the same vision: the heaving earth; the rushing water; the whirls of dust. And then again as it subsided, that date: Friday the 13th of January; Friday the 13th of January; Friday the 13th of January.

He went home to take a tablet and to go to bed. In the next week, despite taking the tablets, it happened to him three times, each in a different place. He could not bring himself to go back to the doctor.

Then gradually the idea that he could see into the future came to him. He felt this dreadful thing was going to happen to his city. He had never been clairvoyant in any way before, but he had a feeling that he was developing strange powers. He tested himself on the TV. He picked three horses. They all won. In the following week he predicted an aeroplane crash, the finding of oil off the coast, and the marriage of a famous film star. He did not know where these events would happen but he just felt they would. Searching through the newspaper feverishly each morning he found that each of the predicted events had happened.

+ + + +

He needed no more proof. He had been given the power to warn the city of a terrible earthquake. What would be the best way of warning it?

The police? He went round to his local police station. They listened to his story, thanked him, gave him a cup of coffee, and brought him home in a police car. He could see they thought he was mad. Perhaps he was, but even as he thought this the vision returned again.

What else could he do? The newspapers? He rang the city paper. A young girl answered the phone, thanked him and said she would inform the editor. He searched the paper for a week but nothing was printed. What could he do now? There were only seven days to go.

He made some placards for himself: THE END OF OUR CITY: 13TH JANUARY. He paraded down the main street.

He did not get far. A police car picked him up and asked him for his licence. How could he get one quickly, he asked. It would take three weeks, they told him.

But the advertising idea stuck in his mind; he would advertise in the local paper. He mapped out an advert:

THE END OF OUR CITY
TERRIBLE EARTHQUAKE PREDICTED
JANUARY THE 13TH
Otis Cornblower

If the advertising manager had not been ill, it would never have been printed. But a young newcomer was in charge and it did. There were five days to go.

+ + + +

People read it and in the main took no notice of it. But then local radio saw it and a disc-jockey put it in his programme for a joke. TV picked it up from there and as they were short of news thought it would be fun to interview this crank with the funny name.

There were four days to go when Mr Otis Cornblower appeared on TV. Audiences saw a rather rude reporter unable to make fun of a quietly dressed and spoken man who insisted that an earthquake was going to take place. Before the programme was over people were on the phone wanting to know what they should do.

With three days to go it was now the second headline in newspapers and the TV stations kept it up. Experts were called who poo-pooed the idea. But one of them let slip that the city was on a structural fault which had just been discovered by his university. By now several nervous old ladies were moving out. These added to the building panic by being interviewed on TV.

Two days before the 13th the Mayor took a hand. He declared that he personally would be on the beach for a picnic for the whole day of the 13th. But his broadcast did not have the effect it wanted. 'More fool him', was the comment of those blocking the roads in a massive traffic jam. He had to return to the TV to explain that the city would break down if key workers left. It was to no avail; the exodus continued.

+ + + +

On Friday the 13th of January it was estimated that over half the population had left. The day dawned heavy with thunder which caused more to leave who had been undecided and another jam on the roads. The clouds built up with the rising sun, stifling the city in a cloak of heat. Few people were on the streets and most of the shops were closed. There was only a skeleton train and bus service.

But as noon approached the clouds suddenly lifted and a glorious afternoon followed enjoyed by the Mayor and his friends on the beach. There was no earthquake as Friday the 13th slid into Saturday the 14th.

Jamming the roads and looking very foolish the people returned. Their foolishness turned to anger when they discovered that many of their homes had been burgled and shops looted. There was an outcry against Otis Cornblower. But where was he?

He was found at a mountain resort two hundred miles away some three weeks later trying to grow a beard as a disguise. On the Mayor's orders a doctor examined him. He was declared in need of treatment. He was moved to the city's mental hospital where he continued to have visions.

Life in the city returned to normal and talk of the incident gradually died. Soon even the newspapers ceased to give medical bulletins on Mr Cornblower.

+ + + +

As the thirteenth of the following year approached a newspaper article reminded the city of its foolishness. People laughed and joked.

Six years later it was forgotten. No journalist noticed Friday the 13th of January again creeping up on the calendar. In the mental home Otis Cornblower was known as Old Quaky to the inmates of the ward because he was still having his visions.

The day was again a scorcher. Picnics were taking place along the entire length of the beach. Shoppers packed the city from end to end. Then there was a sound like the fluttering of a giant bird and the ground lifted.

An Air Force pilot on a training exercise had the best view. Before he climbed rapidly to escape the tremendous turbulence and the dust he saw the city's main street split from end to end and eight more large cracks shoot out from the Central Park like wheel spokes; then the skyscrapers toppled like toy building bricks.

But it was the tidal wave that killed most of the inhabitants of the city. It swept in at a height of twenty feet within minutes of the quake, surging over the flat areas of the city like the tide encroaching on a child's sandcastle.

The mental hospital was on a hill. It was one of the few buildings untouched by the quake.

Think It Over

What happened to Mr Cornblower just before he had his vision?

Who could he talk to about his experience? Why?

Was Mr Cornblower eager to tell the doctor his story? How do you know?

What did the doctor think Mr Cornblower was suffering from?

Did the doctor think it necessary to keep a continual check on Mr Cornblower? How can you tell?

What happened when Mr Cornblower walked in the park?

Why do you think he did not go back to the doctor?

What made him really believe that he had seen a true vision?

What did the police do when he went to see them?

Why could he not carry the placards in the street?

How did it happen that his advertisement got printed?

How did he come to appear on TV?

What helped to make people believe in Mr Cornblower's story?

How many people left the city as a result of it?

How did the Mayor try to calm the situation?

What effect did it have?

What suggested something might happen on the predicted day?

Why were so many homes and shops burgled?

Where had Mr Cornblower gone? Why?

What made people forget about him?

What was the worst part of the earthquake?

What is odd about the end of the story?

Do You Know?

How can you guess Mr Cornblower is a rather delicate kind of man?

What has made you dizzy?

What causes earthquakes? Do they happen everywhere or only in special parts of the world?

Is there a way of judging whether you are overweight or underweight? Where can you find out the scale of weight for your height?

Do you think it is possible to foretell the future? Have you ever had the feeling that something would happen on a particular day?

Do you read your horoscope in the paper? What has it predicted for today or this week?

Can any of your family pick out winners in horse races better than others?

Did Otis Cornblower have enough proof from his predictions?

List all the things you can think of that require a licence.

Is there a TV interviewer you like? Is there one you dislike?
Are there things that should not be shown in the news?
   What are your views?
Would you have left the city? Why?
What is a skeleton train and bus service?

Using Words

Write down other names for strong winds besides a
   tornado.
A subway in England is generally a pedestrian walk under a
   busy road or railway. What is a subway in America?
A person who sees into the future is called a clair. . . .
Write out the months of the year in order. Are the spellings
   right?
'They poo-pooed the idea.' What is another way of saying
   this?
Exodus. What does this mean? Where does it come from?
What is the difference between a burglar and a looter?
In England what name is generally given to a skyscraper?
'Disappeared' How many words where 'dis' is added to
   another word can you think of? Check the spellings or
   look them up in a dictionary.

Write Now

In play-form write out the interview Mr Cornblower had on
   TV.
In play-form write out what the sergeaï.t says to one of his
   men just after Otis Cornblower has gone out of the police
   station.
Imagine that you are able to predict the future. Is it a plea-
   sant gift or an unpleasant one? What would happen?
Make a list of the key workers in a city.

You and a friend have walked off the motorway into a small town. It is completely deserted. Write about what happens and why it is deserted.

Write the pilot's report when he gets back to base.

Describe, in a short paragraph, a hot day on a beach just before a thunderstorm.

You are one of the rescue team helping the victims of an earthquake. Write your diary for one day.

The Curse of the DuCuthberts

Lord Basil DuCuthbert was a brave man in all respects. On the rugby field he had been known as a fearless wing-forward. He had also won a Blue for boxing. Now that he was older and had given up those sports he had put his energies into the hunting field. Some of his riding in order to be first at the kill was already a legend. He could coax a horse over the highest hedges and the deepest ditches.

But he was approaching his fortieth birthday with some apprehension. His fear was not outward. Indeed only that morning he had been laughing and joking with his wife at breakfast; a fact that the butler had remarked upon. No, it was a fear that broke into his dreams and woke him at night.

The reason was not a dread of middle age; it held no terrors for one so fit. It was the fact that his father, Lord George DuCuthbert, had disappeared in mysterious circumstances on his fortieth birthday. He was never found. There was a theory that he had been killed by a gorilla which was discovered wandering in the grounds of DuCuthbert Park. This gorilla was a fearsome beast and it had savaged the police marksman before it fell to the ground. But no body of Lord George was ever found. The mystery was deepened by the fact that no gorilla had been reported as missing from any zoo.

+ + + +

As a young man Lord George DuCuthbert had been a keen hunter of big game in Africa. He had often told his son, Basil, hair-raising tales of the African jungle. His son had loved them all but his favourite was the tale of the Oratuga Diamond. Lord George needed no prompting to retell this tale; it was his favourite as well.

Several days' march from his base camp he had come upon a clearing in the jungle, in the middle of which was a native hut. Outside the hut was a huge and fearsome gorilla.

The native bearers dropped their loads and fled back into the jungle. But Lord George sank to his knee to take steady aim. With saliva dripping from its lips the gorilla came towards him. His first shot hit it in the chest yet it still came on. The second went through its neck yet still it advanced. It was not until the third went between its eyes that it stumbled to the ground.

He went carefully towards it. It lay in the long grass. The look it had given him remained with him all his days. Although in its death agony, its eyes blazed with hatred. It had stretched up an arm, too, and scratched Lord George on his left cheek. It marked him for life.

+ + + +

As he stemmed the flow of blood from his face Lord George saw that the gorilla was tethered by strong creepers to both neck and legs. It could not have reached him or his bearers anyway.

He now went towards the hut. No one had come out of it so he had concluded that it was empty. He drew back the reed curtain in the doorway. There in the middle of a mud floor on newly cut leaves was the most magnificent diamond he had ever seen. He picked it up; it must have weighed half a pound. Strangely, it was beautifully cut as if by European craftsmen. He counted the facets; there were forty of them.

Some of the native bearers had by now returned. The head man told him that he should put the diamond back and leave at once. He said he had heard of a curse on such a diamond. But Lord George only laughed at this native superstition and would not give up the rich prize his gun had won. He ordered his bearers to return with him to camp.

There was great excitement among the white members of

the expedition when they saw the diamond. They said that Lord George must go back to England at once and show off his prize. He resolved to return to the coast and thence to England the next day.

+ + + +

That night he slept with the diamond on him. He awoke to a noise and was just in time to dodge a long steel blade coming for his throat. He wrestled in the darkness and soon overcame a small figure. Lighting the lamp he found that his attacker was a pigmy witch doctor who kept pointing at the pillow under which the diamond lay. Lord George called the head bearer who talked with the witch doctor. He explained that the diamond was the Oratuga Diamond, a sacred stone, and that it must be returned to its owners, the pigmy tribe. If this was not done the spirits of the jungle would seek a terrible revenge on the thief.

Lord George watched the witch doctor's rolling eyes and waving arms. He started to laugh at him. His friends came in and were told the tale. Soon there was general laughter among the white members of the expedition while the native bearers round the fire showed in the glinting of their eyes their fear. Finally the witch-doctor was whipped out of the camp by Lord George himself. He still laughed when he retold this tale in England.

+ + + +

Although he had enjoyed the tale as a young boy, Lord Basil felt a tremble run through him when his father laughed as he grew older. He remembered too how his father had told the tale for the last time the night before his mysterious disappearance. The scar on his left cheek had seemed to glow as his face became redder and redder with laughter, causing Lord Basil to finger the birth mark on his own left cheek. 'Yes, you've got the mark of the gorilla too,' laughed Lord George.

+ + + +

And here he was now with his own fortieth birthday approaching. The diamond was in a bank. He had not dared to keep it in the house like Lord George. Once a year, on his birthday, he went to gaze on the diamond. He did not want to go, but something compelled him. Each time he felt his face go red like his father's and his left cheek tingle as the diamond seemed to burn into his skin.

He could not sleep. He resolved that it was stupid to worry so over a stone. He would not see it tomorrow however compelled he felt to go; he would have it returned to the country from whence it came. This helped him sleep. But it was not a peaceful one; it was a sleep of nightmares. Great fronds brushed his face, creepers tripped him, shrieks and cries echoed through his brain, strange smells made him feel he was choking.

He was thankful to wake and see the dawn light coming through the curtain. But he did not feel himself. He felt very heavy and befuddled as if he had been drinking heavily.

There was a knock at the door. That would be his wife coming from her room. He tried to say, 'Come in,' but he could only grunt.

'Happy birthday, darling,' said his wife coming in. Then a look of horror filled her face. She dropped the present she was carrying and ran, screaming, from the room.

'What is the matter with her?' thought Lord Basil. The thought came to him very slowly. But he knew she was his wife and was acting in a strange way.

He lay, listening to running feet below and doors opening and closing. He wanted to get out of bed but he felt so heavy and his limbs did not seem his own. He must drag himself awake and see what the fuss was about.

Then there was a man in the doorway. It was his gardener. The fool was raising a gun at him. He put out an arm to stop him. The arm was black and hairy, not his own at all. Then there was this pain in his chest as the gun was fired. He must kill this fool who was shooting at him. The gun went off again causing him to put his hand to his cheek. He must rip this creature to bits. Then his head seemed to explode.

Think It Over

Was Lord Basil cruel to his horses? What word gives you a
   clue?
Why was Lord Basil afraid of his fortieth birthday?
How had his father, Lord George, died?
Why had it been a bit unsporting for Lord George to shoot
   the gorilla?
Why were the natives uneasy when the diamond was taken
   back to the camp?
What was odd about the witch-doctor?
What did he say would happen if the diamond was not
   returned?
What strange compulsion came over Lord Basil on each
   birthday?
What decision helped him to sleep?
Why did his wife scream when she saw him?
What might the gorilla, shot by Lord George, have been?

Do You Know?

What does a Blue at sport mean?
Name some of the positions in a rugby team.
What do you understand by middle age?
Has a wild animal ever escaped in your area? If so, what
   happened?
Who was the gorilla shot by the police?
Why are gorillas so frightening to most people? Do they
   normally attack people? Find out what you can about
   them and write a short report.
What does 'King Kong' do when it escapes in New York?
Diamonds are not usually weighed by the pound. What
   weight is used?
What is the significance of the forty facets? What is a facet?
Should Lord George have taken the diamond? Why?

Do you know any other treasures with a curse on them?

What is a pigmy?

Who might the pigmy witch-doctor have worshipped?

Why might Lord Basil have a mark on his left cheek?

Which of the two Lords is more sensitive?

What is the greatest mystery that has happened in your house?

About what date might this story have taken place? How would Lord George have travelled in those days?

How could the curse be broken so that Lord Basil's son did not suffer the same fate?

Using Words

Make up some suitable surnames for posh people. They could be comic ones like Lord Snooty.

Give two other words for 'apprehension'.

What does 'already a legend' mean?

Make a list of animals that are 'Big Game'. Make another of 'Small Game'.

Combine these sentences into one long sentence and then check your version with the sentence in the story: 'He was several days' march from his base camp. He came upon a clearing in the jungle. In the middle of the clearing was a native hut.'

'Tethered' means to tie up an animal. What single word means to tie up a boat?

Give one word to describe how each of these animals walks: a cat, an elephant and a horse.

Make a list of words from twentieth to fortieth. Check all the spellings.

Write Now

Write a story about a big game hunter who comes across a

very strange animal.

There are many folk tales about people who can change into animals and change back again. Write one of your own about a werewolf.

Where are diamonds found? How are they cut and polished? Find out and write a short article about it.

If you were writing this story as a television play, you would have to divide it into scenes. Which scenes would you use? Would you add any scenes? Would you start where the story starts? Make a plan of the scenes you would use.

How would you feel if you found a gorilla or strange animal in your bedroom? Write a few sentences about it.

Make a list of precious stones.

What noises can you hear at night? Make a list. What noises might you hear in the jungle?

A Voice Without Sound

Susan flopped down on the edge of the bath with her mouth open, staring at the white scrawl on the bathroom mirror. John, her brother, banged on the door and demanded, 'How much longer are you going to be?'

She continued to gaze, speechlessly, until, when he banged again and shouted, she managed to croak, 'Just a minute! Hang on.'

'Oh, come on, for Heaven's sake!' he groaned. It hardly registered. Reluctantly she picked up the mashed tube of toothpaste and looked at it closely. Just a few seconds before, that tube had risen waveringly into the air all of its own accord and written, 'Hello, Susan.' shakily across the glass.

'How on earth—?' she murmured.

'What are you muttering about now?' John banged. 'Come on!'

'I *can't* have done it. But how else—?'

—It was me.—Fear like the legs of a million woodlice danced all over her skin.

+ + + +

'Who?' Her head darted from side to side. She was quite alone except, apparently, for the invisible owner of a voice that made no actual sound.

—Me—said the voice, weirdly, triumphantly, speaking directly to her mind. She fumblingly unlocked the door, passed John without a word or a glance, went into her bedroom and shut the door. His scowl changed to a puzzled look; he opened his mouth, then shrugged and slammed into the bathroom.

Susan began to dress apprehensively. She knew, without

quite knowing how, that the thing had followed her into the room and she did not want to stir it up by doing something incautious.

—I bet you can't guess what I am.— Wide-eyed, pale and with slack lips, her face stared back at her from the dressing-table mirror. Automatically, the hand that held the brush went on moving across her hair. Nothing had been spoken aloud. But she had not thought that sentence, either.

—Imagination? A hallucination?—she thought. Though weren't hallucinations just things you could see, or could you hear them as well?

—Wrong—The voice that had no sound seemed, all the same, flat, a bit harsh and more than a little mad.

—I'm dreaming—she thought, without hope.

—Guess again.—

—You're a ghost?—

—Good. Much nearer. I'm a poltergeist.—

—Poltergeist?—

—An elemental spirit. You usually find us in places where there is a girl between the age of ten and—where there is a teen-age girl. Like you. We have the power of moving objects about. Pictures fall off walls, plates smash on the floor, ornaments shoot across the room.—

—I have heard of them. But they don't *talk* to the girls. I don't believe it. You're just in my mind.—

—You watch!—

Susan squealed, 'Don't do that!' but the bedside lamp took off, turned upside down, flew a yard and crashed on the floor.

—Smashed the bulb.—The mind-voice seemed more pleased than otherwise.

'What's going on? Why did you smear toothpaste all over the bathroom mirror, you nit?' John blundered in. 'Who're you shouting at?' He saw the lamp. 'Clumsy devil. You'll cop it, if that bulb's broken.' He bent down. 'And it is. Have you seen my shirt?'

This was madder than ever. The last thing she needed at the moment was one of John's pointless conversations. 'How would your shirt be in here?' she demanded. 'Get out, anyway. Can't you see I'm getting dressed?'

'Getting? You are dressed. How did you smash the lamp?'

'Never mind. Buzz off.' She pushed him towards the door, making him stagger.

'Watch it!' He aimed a fake punch at her stomach. 'Who'd want to be in your room? It niffs in here. Scent! Yerch!' He made a face and was gone.

+ + + +

—You will be glad I came. One of my functions is to protect you. And he doesn't treat you as he should.—

—John's all right.—She was suddenly defensive.

—No, he isn't. I know what is necessary here.—

It was an odd sensation. It had nothing to do with sight or hearing. There was absolutely nothing to see or hear—or touch, if it came to that, but, quite suddenly, she knew that the thing had gone. From the next room came the sound of a crash and a shout. Then, like a shadow, a breeze, an odd heaviness on her mind, it was back.

—There!—it stated.—Done. You may tell him why, though there's no point in it.—

She went out on to the landing. John came out of his room, rubbing the backs of his legs with both hands.

'Blinking chair!' he grumbled. 'I was tying my tie in the mirror and, when I stepped back, I fell over a chair right behind me.' He stood still, fixing her with a hot, suspicious stare. 'You slipped in and moved it there.'

'No.' She shook her head.

'Hm. Suppose I'd have seen you in the mirror. Must have moved it there myself without thinking.'

She swallowed and blurted before her courage could desert her, 'It was a poltergeist.'

'Very funny, our kid,' he growled and went on downstairs.

—What did you do that for?—she demanded indignantly.

—A punishment.—

—It was a stupid thing to do. He might have really hurt himself.—

—Nonsense—

—It's not nonsense. You must be crazy. I didn't ask you to do it. I don't think having a poltergeist is a good idea at all.—

—You're a child. What can you know about it?—

'Oh—push off!' said Susan aloud.

—What?—

'Shove off!' she repeated.

—If you're going to be like that—. I'll be around when you want me.—

+ + + +

And it had gone. The presence that, evidently, only she could feel and hear, the weight in her mind had left her completely. She followed John down and ate her breakfast in a very thoughtful silence.

The thing, even in its absence, haunted her all day. Looking back, as she lay in bed that night, she remembered school as one long telling-off for being absent-minded, dull and clumsy. She had been too preoccupied to do much homework and that bit she had done badly. She felt resentment and regret. Could it protect her? If she had had the poltergeist with her, she might have taught Old Blewitt in maths not to be so sarcastic and Mrs Parker in cookery not to shout so much. She had been too hasty. She wished it would come back.

+ + + +

—I thought you would,—it purred. She started so much that the bed-springs bounced beneath her.

—I don't want you whispering about in my head, now,—she told it.—I needed you during the day. I don't even want you hanging about in this room. If I can sense that you're there, I won't be able to get to sleep.—

—Don't worry. I can go—elsewhere. But you want me back?—

—I suppose so.—

—You are inviting me of your own free will and accord?—

—If you like. Yes.—

—Then the pact is made. Look for me to be with you tomorrow.—

And it had gone once more. There was more than the shadow of a doubt in her mind which might have kept her awake but she was tired enough to go to sleep almost immediately and she was glad of her decision next day, at first.

Waiting in the dinner queue was bad enough without having people push in ahead of you with their trays. Fred Dawes, Dai Rhys and Big Martin did just that. She and Sally started to protest but were shouted at and pushed about for doing it. Fred Dawes pulled her hair.

Susan's furious internal promptings seemed hardly necessary. The three boys had got their trays filled and then, as Fred turned back to jeer, his tray flew up, sending meat and potato into his face and gravy and custard down his blazer. He yelped and reeled, cannoning into Big Martin and knocking his tray out of his hands. Dai Rhys, jumping to avoid its contents, skidded in the mess on the floor and fell sprawling with his trayful covering a sizeable expanse of wall. Mr Payne on dinner duty, made more bad-tempered than usual by all the laughter and noise, ordered them to get buckets and mops and they had to clear everything up. By the time they had finished, all they got to eat was odds and ends.

Except for the incident with Mrs Parker in cookery, the afternoon was uneventful and Susan had not asked for that herself. Mrs Parker was tut-tutting and calling Susan names as usual when a tin fell off a shelf behind her and hit her on the head. No one dared to laugh. No one noticed that the tin had not dropped vertically but must have travelled some distance through the air to get where it had, either.

Walking home from the bus alone that afternoon, Susan felt confused and uneasy. Possession of this new power had lost a good deal of its attraction. She could not threaten anyone with it and she would not do that even if she could. What did concern her was that the poltergeist seemed to have very little sense of proportion; from the look on Parker's face, that tin had really hurt. Her greatest worry, however, was herself. She had enjoyed the downfall of the boys and, for a moment, Mrs Parker's pain. Obviously her helper was a spiteful thing, perhaps dangerous. Was she becoming like it? She ought to do something about that. She knew that the thing, invisibly, noiselessly, was flitting along not far away.

—You mustn't go too far.—she challenged it.

—Too far?—Was it mocking her?—You have seen nothing of my powers, yet, child.—

—Well, I don't want you getting rough with people. I don't want anyone hurt. As a matter of fact, I don't want you to do anything, unless I ask for it.—

—You will give the orders?—

—Listen!—There had been something in its tone that showed her things were not going as they should.—If you don't behave yourself, I don't want you.—It did not answer at once. She had a very odd feeling that, if she could see it, it would have an evil smile on its face.

—That's not for you to decide now, Susan.—It was gloating.

—Why not?—She was suddenly quite frightened.—Hey! Look! If you're going to be like that, I don't want you. You can go away. Now.—

—You can't send me away, Susan. That time is past. You invited me to stay. We made a little pact. You remember?—It seemed absolutely sure of itself, triumphant and jeering.

—I don't want you.—

—What a pity. But you've got me—until I decide to go.—

+ + + +

She felt cold and shocked. Believed or not, she had to tell someone. Her mother was clearing up in the kitchen when she got in.

'Don't just stand around, love,' she said. 'Put the kettle on for some tea. I've been washing all day. There's something wrong with the machine. Still, I've got them all out now.' She looked out of the back window at the long line of clothes. 'I should think the rain will keep off. It looks as if we're going to have a fine, still evening.'

Susan put the kettle on, wondering how to begin. 'Maybe it was a poltergeist that made the washing machine go wrong,' she suggested.

'Very likely.' Her mother smiled.

'Do you think there are such things?'

'I've no idea.'

'What would you do, if we had one in the house?'

'I don't know.'

'I think I've got one.'

The confession did not at all have the effect she intended. 'Have you?' asked her mother idly. 'How do you know?'

'It talks to me.'

This time her mother looked at her a little harder. 'You mean—like a little friend?'

'No, not a friend.'

+ + + +

'Oh! Heavens above! Just look at that!' Her mother pushed past her and out of the kitchen door. Something was dragging the clothes off the line, sending them tossing and jerking all over the garden to snag on bushes or sprawl in the mud. Susan ran out to help and said no more. What would have been the point? The poltergeist would have other ways of keeping her quiet and a snatch of conversation she heard later made her glad that she had not said too much.

She had been in bed unable to sleep. That sly, husky voice kept trying to intrude into her mind and eventually she crept downstairs for a book to read. With a torch under the bedclothes, she could keep her attention occupied and shut out the slithery whispering. As she passed the living room door on her way back up, they were turning off the television and she heard her mother say, 'Susan was funny when she came in.'

'How?' her father asked.

'She said she had a little friend that talked to her.'

'So?'

'Well—I mean—she's too old for that. It's what kids do when they're three or four. They imagine they have a rabbit or another little child that goes round with them. Something like that. Susan's much too old for that sort of stuff. She'll be thirteen next.'

'I did know that, dear. Would have been difficult not to these last few days. But I wouldn't worry about her little friend. It's probably something she had to do for her English homework. They're very fond of this imaginative writing, nowadays.'

'She didn't say so.'

'Shall we take her to see a psychiatrist, then? He'd maybe shoot her into Wycliffe. And John, too, if we asked him really nicely.'

'Oh—you never take anything I say seriously!'

+ + + +

In spite of the joke, Susan's blood chilled as she crept upstairs. Wycliffe was for mental patients only. She read until the torch dimmed and, when she put it out, her worries and the thought of that evil spirit lurking in the darkness made her nerves so raw that it was almost impossible to sleep. She must have dropped off at last but she was tired and edgy in the morning.

When her father made another of his feeble jokes, she snapped at him so that he shouted at her. There was no warning from the voice in her head but her father's anger was cut short as he yelped and flinched. A fork had sprung up from the table, catching him on the cheek sharply enough to leave white dints, flushing to red.

'What's the matter now?' Her mother came in with more toast.

'This thing!' Her father picked up the fork and flung it indignantly down on the table. 'It just flew up at me. A bit higher and I would have got it in the eye.' He rubbed his cheek. 'It came with some force.' He examined the faint, pink smear on his finger. 'Broken the skin.'

'Hardly.' Her mother looked at his cheek. 'You probably had the end of it off the table and hit it with your hand to make it spin up.'

'I didn't.'

'I'll bet you did. You were carrying on enough at Susan. I'll bet you were waving your arms about as you do.'

'Never. Anyway, I'm off. And you just stop being so cheeky!' He pointed a reproving finger at Susan and left.

Susan went out, too, without another word. The unpredictable and savage lunge at her father's eye had made her feel weak and sick. She could not bear to speak to the thing until she had her coat on and was outside.

—That was a terrible thing to do.—

—That was nothing. I can do more than that, much, much more, now.—

—But I don't want you to! I want you to leave me alone.—

—That's likely,—it sneered.—Hadn't you noticed how, the longer I'm with you, the more my power grows? My power and my pleasure. I shall not leave. Not after your invitation.—

—It wasn't an invitation.—

It ignored her.—Soon now, I shall be able to do great

things through you. Really terrible things.—It was full of a mad, evil glee and Susan could stand no more.

'No!' she shouted and began to run, as if that way she could escape.

+ + + +

Brakes squealed; she yelled and leapt aside. The car rocked to a halt. If she had jumped the other way, she would have been under it.

'You little fool!' the driver raged at her. 'Haven't you any more sense at your age?' They stared at each other. Susan was beyond speech. 'Let it be a lesson to you,' he said more calmly. 'Be more careful in future.' He pulled his body back into the car and slammed the door.

—He might have killed you!—the secret voice snarled.—Then where would I have been?'—

'Don't!' Susan cried but the car was moving, gathering speed. From behind a privet hedge, as if driven by some huge, freak wind, a dustbin lid sailed to crash into the car's windscreen. The brakes squealed again, too late; the car ran on to the pavement and stopped with a splintering of glass and a rending of metal, as it ran into a gatepost. Two men further down the road began to run; the driver got shakily out and stood with bowed head leaning on the roof. Doors along the street opened and people began to come out and stare.

Susan stumbled away, taking that evil influence with her, her eyes blurred by tears of fright and frustration. She made no further attempt to plead with the thing. It was useless. All that morning until after break, school was dim around her. She knew people were looking at her strangely but she was hardly aware of them. What was real was this nightmare in which she was alone with something as deaf to all pleading as thunder and more ferocious than a panther.

Mild Mrs Armstrong woke her from it. She must already have spoken to Susan two or three times but the first she knew of it was when Mrs Armstrong shook her shoulder and said something sharp.

'Leave me alone!' cried Susan, blindly brushing her away as all the pent-up emotion broke out. 'Leave me alone, can't you?'

'Susan! Get hold of yourself! What's the matter with you?' Flustered, Mrs Armstrong replaced the glasses that Susan's flailing arm had dislodged from her nose. Susan burst into tears and put her head on the desk.

'She's been like that all morning, Miss,' someone said.

'Susan?' said Mrs Armstrong.

'Yes?' Susan buried her face in her handkerchief, ashamed to meet any of their eyes.

'This isn't like you at all. You'd better go along to the Sick Room. I'll be along in a minute to see what all this is about.'

Meekly, sobbing, Susan went. What did it matter? It had been almost the end of the lesson anyway and Mrs Armstrong came along a few minutes later. Susan got up from the bunk on which she had been sitting and went out into the corridor.

'Now, what is this all about?' asked Mrs Armstrong crisply.

'I've been worried.'

The Sick Room was next to the Headmaster's study. He chose this moment to come out, stopped and asked, 'What seems to be the trouble, Mrs Armstrong?' She explained and he turned to Susan. 'Worried? Is that any excuse? What about?'

'A poltergeist.' She could not stop herself blurting the word out.

'A what—?' The expression on his face was too much. She began to laugh. She could not help it. She was laughing and crying at the same time until it hurt. He smacked her hard across the face. She gasped and was silent. There was an enormous silence everywhere. But nothing happened to him.

+ + + +

'Go and sit down in the Sick Room,' Mr Formby said mildly. 'We'd better let her go home,' he addressed Mrs Armstrong. 'I'll ring her mother. Is there someone you can send with her?' Mrs Armstrong closed the door on her and their voices were only a mumble.

—He struck you—the voice brooded.—A direct challenge to my power. So I must not be hasty. I must consider the punishment. Ah, yes! Tomorrow.—

—What are you going to do?—A storm of despair and panic raged round her.

—I shall burn him alive.—The leathery soundlessness was full of delighted certainty.—There are too many in this place who would harm you. I shall lock all the doors and set it on fire.—

+ + + +

Horror made Susan too numb to reply. Linda Dawson, whom she did not know well, came then and they went home together. Linda tried to talk but Susan had no heart to say much and it was Linda who explained things to her mother before she left.

'You'd better go straight up and get into bed,' her mother advised. 'Do you want the doctor?'

'I'm all right.' Susan shook her head. 'I'm tired.'

All she wanted was to be left alone. But she was tired. She felt dead, beyond explanations or tears.

'Get undressed then and hop into bed quickly. I'll bring you a hot-water bottle as soon as you're in. Cup of tea?'

'No, thanks.' Susan dragged her way upstairs and got into bed. Her mother put a hot-water bottle at her feet, made her take two aspirins and tucked her in like a baby. 'You have a little sleep,' she ordered. 'We'll talk about it later.'

Exhaustion covered Susan in a cloud and, before, she could even think about it, she was asleep.

It was mid-afternoon when she awoke and the terror was there gripping her savagely.—You can't! You mustn't!—she implored.

—I will,—it promised.

—People may be killed. Badly injured—

—Oh, yes!—

She thought of priests who might rid her of the evil spirit. But it would know ways of stopping that. If she herself were dead, would the thing have any power? Abruptly she put her head under the bedclothes and pulled them tightly round her ears.

—Please don't do it,—she begged.—Tomorrow's my birthday.—It was a silly thing to say and it would not help but the fact that it was her birthday did make things worse.

After a moment she put her head out and sat up, frowning. She had an odd feeling that she had profoundly disturbed the thing in some way.

+ + + +

—How old will you be?—There was no longer any triumph in it when it broke the long pause.

—Thirteen—

—When?—It was definitely anxious and angry.

—Tomorrow—

—No, you fool. At what time?—

—How do I know?—

Her sense of it had sharpened. She could almost imagine it, prowling like an animal in silent, baffled rage. Desperate as she was, her brain was still enough alive to realise that she had stumbled on something very important indeed. She threw off the bedclothes and ran downstairs.

'Mum! When was I born?'

'Susan! Are you feeling all right, now? You look a lot better. And you must know when you were born.'

'No, Mum. At what time of day. When exactly am I thirteen?'

'I can remember that well enough.' Her mother smiled. 'Between eight and nine in the morning.'

Susan fled upstairs and sat on the bed clasping her knees.

—That's it!—she challenged.—You can't stay with me

after I'm thirteen, can you? Not a moment. That's why you're so disappointed, you nasty thing, aren't you?—

It was there but it made no reply.—Can you?—she insisted. It did not answer.—We'll just see, then—she taunted it.

And yet she could not be absolutely sure. The only way to prove it was to go to school and take the chance. It was difficult to get through the evening, difficult to sleep and even her pleasure in her presents in the morning could not entirely drown the rising tide of the other excitement.

+ + + +

She sat on the back seat of the bus, facing the pavement, quivering with fear and expectancy. It was twenty-five minutes to nine. Three stops to go to school. Past the Guildhall, right down Waterburn Road, checked at the lights. The sweltering heaviness of the thing was still with her.

And it was still there when they stopped outside the Roxy. Had she been quite wrong? She gnawed a knuckle. Noisily a mother and daughter came down from upstairs. Susan looked. The woman was angry, the girl a year or two younger than Susan.

'Never seen anyone like you in all my born days!' the woman scolded. 'Go on—get off!' She pushed the girl forward.

In that instant the heaviness left Susan's mind. The evil spirit had gone. She had never been so certain or so happy about anything in her life before. The bell rang a chime of victory and release and the bus moved on.

In the next moment, Susan sat transfixed. The mother had paused at the stop, the better to scold and shake her daughter. A litter-bin rose impossibly from its anchorage at the post, reversed itself and descended to cover the woman's head, cascading banana peel, plastic bags and crumpled chip papers down her shoulders. On the girl's face was the horror and astonishment of one who feels an unseen presence whose harsh, mad voice only she can hear. Then the bus left them behind.

Think It Over

Why did Susan gaze speechlessly at the mirror?

What did the voice do when she went from the bathroom to the bedroom?

How did the poltergeist feel about John?

What did it do to him?

Why was Susan's work bad the next day?

What was her big mistake?

What was the first thing it did for her? And the second?

What unpleasant news did it give her?

What did she decide to do?

How did it prevent her from giving away its secret?

What frightened her about her parents' conversation later that night?

Who did the poltergeist attack next? Why?

What did it do when the motorist shouted at her?

Why did the headmaster hit her?

What was the poltergeist going to do in revenge for that?

What happened to the poltergeist in the end?

Do You Know?

What would you do, if you heard a voice that no one else could hear? Would you tell other people? Why?

Have any unusual accidents happened in your home? How did you explain them?

What do you know about poltergeists? What are they supposed to do?

Would you make any changes in the dining arrangements at your school? If so, what?

Did you ever imagine that you had a secret companion? If you did, what was it like?

If you have a brother or sister, how much do you quarrel,

fight or insult each other? When was the last time you had a quarrel? What happened?

Was the headmaster's way of dealing with Susan's hysterics a good one? What do you think? What would you have done?

Does Susan's father take much interest in his daughter? Give some reasons from the story for your answer.

Was this story too long? Did it gain from being of fuller length? Do you prefer long or short stories?

Using Words

'Hang on!' How many ways can you think of saying this?

'He . . . slammed into the bathroom.' Rewrite the sentence to describe the way he would have gone in if (a) he had gone in in the normal way, (b) he had gone in very quietly, (c) he had gone in very happily.

'You'll cop it.' How would an adult, a teacher for instance, say the same thing?

'Fear like the legs of a million woodlice danced all over her skin.' How would you describe fear? 'Fear is like . . .'

'Our kid' What various things do you call your brother or sister?

When you are very upset and laughing and crying at the same time, you are in hys. . . .

'The rain will keep off' Use 'keep on', 'keep out,' 'keep together', 'keep up with', in sentences of your own.

What are you, if you are apprehensive?

Write Now

Describe a room after a poltergeist has been at work.

Are you absent-minded? Write a few sentences about an absent-minded man or woman.

In play-form write out the conversation the poltergeist

might have had with the girl it visited next *OR* write a conversation that often goes on in your house.

Write a story in which you have a friendly spirit which no one else but you can see and which has magic power. What would you get it to do?

How observant are you? If you walk to school, list the streets you walk along. If you go by bus, train or car, list the important places you pass. Compare your list with those who make a similar journey.